Sekani's Solution

Tito Banda

Luviri Books no. 12

Mzuzu

2018

Published by
Mzuni Press
P/Bag 201 Luwinga
Mzuzu 2

ISBN   978-99960-98-10-9
eISBN 978-99960-98-11-6

The Mzuni Press is represented outside Africa by:
African Books Collective Oxford (order@africanbookscollective.com)

www.mzunipress.blogspot.com
www.africanbookscollective.com

To the loving memory of my parents
Hezron Banda and Keti Nyamkandawire

Preface to the Second Edition

Although in this re-issuing of my first novel I have taken the opportunity to improve the presentation of the story, this revised edition of *Sekani's Solution* is very much the same story as the first edition. The changes are largely structural – a few minor adjustments in the narrative here and there and some re-organisation of chapters in a few cases. Therefore, those who enjoyed the first edition can rest assured that, despite these revisions, there really has been no change in the story of one-eyed Andreya Soko and his fiancée Sekani Zuza, the most beautiful girl in the Republic of Dziko.

Tito Banda

CHAPTER ONE

It was well past midnight, but Andreya Soko and his roommate Jarafi Tauzi were still awake in their room at Ginezi Teacher Training College. Lying uncovered in the humid heat of early December, they tossed and turned behind their mosquito nets, half-whispering to each other across the solid darkness of the room. They were too excited to sleep, for the following day the college was closing for the Christmas holidays. Besides sharing at length how each was planning to spend the holidays, the two gossiped endlessly about their experiences in college that term. It had been their first term together.

Andreya rolled over onto his right side in order to face the direction of his room-mate. He yawned – a brief unreal yawn – and then asked his friend: "You wouldn't say Harold Mphande and Sekani Zuza have been on the best of terms this term, would you, Jarafi?"

"There you go again!" Jarafi said with a muffled laugh. "That's about the 96th time you've mentioned Sekani tonight! Is Cupid shooting the arrows?"

"Yes, I do think I'm in love with the girl," Andreya admitted with a sigh.

"You're not the only one, my friend," Jarafi said, and then cleared his throat in a manner intended to tease Andreya.

"You're also in love with her?"

"Not me!" Jarafi said with a quiet laugh. "But quite a few students here are."

"Who and who and who?" Andreya asked with assumed indifference.

"Oh, several guys have made passes at her, including Harold. She's given every one of them the rebuff; hence the sour relationship between her and Harold: He's not one to take a rebuff gracefully."

"How do you know all this, Jarafi?" Andreya inquired, propping himself on his right elbow, no longer able to continue with his pretended indifference.

Jarafi chuckled and said: "This is my second and last year here, isn't it? It's only your first year – your first term, in fact. I should therefore know a lot more about this place than you, shouldn't I? You see, I've been here long enough to establish a very efficient grapevine. It has branches in every room of the girl's dorms!"

"You and your grapevine!" Andreya said with a chuckle. "Tell me more, then."

"What more is there to tell you?" Jarafi said self-assuredly as he hit his net to frighten away a mosquito that was droning in front of his forehead in a vain attempt to enter the netting. "I've told you your admired one has rejected all the suitors so far. She's thus still available. Go ahead and try your luck."

"She sounds tough," Andreya said, grinning into the darkness. "But one can always, as you say, try one's luck. The worst she can do is say no. And I'm sure I can take her rejection with more grace than Harold... My goodness, Harold has become really sour to the girl. You should've seen how he bullied her when the Drama Club went to perform at St. Luke's Teacher Training College two weeks ago: On our way back to Ginezi, he had an argument with her in which he harassed her mercilessly, calling her all sorts of crude names. But she ignored everything with disarming patience. She impresses me as a very self-assured girl. I suppose that's one reason I'm attracted to her."

"Try her, my friend. As you say, the worst she can do is say no. Good luck!"

"Thanks," Andreya said as he resumed his lying position to a twang of springs. "It appears I will need tons of luck! I hope she's going north for the holidays. In which case I will make sure I sit with her on the bus tomorrow."

They fell into a momentary silence during which Jarafi assessed his friend's chances with Sekani. Andreya and the girl certainly had a lot in common, if their choice of clubs was enough indication of that. But there was one thing which, as far as Jarafi could see, right away disqualified Andreya: He was one-eyed. Except for this unfortunate fact, Andreya was quite capable of winning Sekani. He was a steady young man of sound sense, and cheerful in an intelligent way; he was one of the few first-year students who had become so popular with the entire college community that one found it difficult to believe they had been on campus for only three months. On top of all this, he was tall and had a pleasant if not handsome face. And so, had he not lost his left eye in that childhood accident (another boy had accidentally shot an arrow through it), there would be no doubt about Andreya winning his girl. But as it was, Sekani had more eligible suitors to choose from: young men endowed with all the good qualities Andreya possessed – but minus the handicap of being one-eyed. Thus Jarafi didn't think his love-struck friend's chances with the young lady were particularly good, even if one considered the fact that Andreya and Sekani came from the same part of the country, though Jarafi wasn't sure whether they came from the same district.

"By the way, where does she come from?" Jarafi asked. "I know she's from the Northern Province. But which district there?"

"Same district I come from – Katoto."

"I see. Well, let's hope she's going north for her holidays. If she is, I'm sure it will go well for you on the bus. At least you should find it easy to get into conversation with her, as both of you are active members of the Students Christian Organisation, the Drama Club, and the Debating Club."

"I hope that helps. But my immediate problem is how to secure a seat beside her on the bus." He scratched his head where it did not itch.

"Oh, I think we can easily work that out. Her friend and room-mate

7

Eva Midaya should be able to help us with that one. Let me be in charge of that."

"Hey, thanks, mate," Andreya said.

Just then a cock crowed in a nearby village, heralding the approach of a new day. Andreya and Jarafi decided to stop the chatter and try to catch some sleep. They agreed that whoever woke up first in the morning should wake up the other.

*   *   *

At nine o'clock that morning the closing assembly was over. As Andreya stepped out of the door at one end of the assembly hall, he saw Sekani skip down the steps of the door at the other end of the building. She began to run towards the girls' dorms. Andreya's good eye followed her as she ran along lightly, the hem of her red-and-white dress gracefully swishing to and fro across the back of her knees.

As he walked along about twenty metres behind her, Andreya was thinking that Sekani looked prettier than ever that morning. Even after she had disappeared round a bend, he could still mentally see those long, handsomely straight legs. He could still see her large, placid and very round brown eyes; her full lips; her deep-dark hair, so naturally short and kinky, untouched by a hot comb yet well groomed; her pretty round face, naturally earth-brown, the colour of the rest of her....

"Hey, Andreya!" Jarafi said as he caught up with his friend, his voice breaking into Andreya's romantic day-dreaming. "Are you aware the buses are already here?"

"Are they?" Andreya asked with a slight start. Before Jarafi could answer, they turned round a building and two buses parked in front of the dining hall came into view. They were Ufulu Transport Company buses, hired by the Students Union for students bound for the Central and Northern Provinces. "So that's why everybody's been running," Andreya said. He quickened his pace, only to stop after a while. "It appears Sekani's going North, Jarafi," he whispered. "She was the first to come out of Assembly hall."

Jarafi said: "Yes, she is. But not all the way to Katoto. I was talking to Eva in the assembly hall and she said Sekani is going to spend the holidays with her aunt at Mwera."

"That's good enough, Jarafi!" Andreya said, clapping his hands once as he took a short leap for joy into the air. "Oh, I am so glad she's going North! Tell me, what arrangements have you and Eva made regarding my sitting with Sekani on the bus?" he asked with a smile.

"No problem. All's set. You'll only need to follow me. And guess what: Eva says it won't be difficult for you. I think she knows something we don't know!"

"You've got to be joking, Jarafi," Andreya whispered excitedly, staring down at the grinning face of his much shorter friend. "Do you really think Eva might have meant that Sekani is also interested in me?"

"Andreya," Jarafi said in a conspiratorial tone, "if Eva, Sekani's room-mate and closest friend, says it won't be difficult for you, one may be forgiven for drawing certain conclusions."

They ran the rest of the way to their dorm.

CHAPTER TWO

"That's me ready!" Andreya jovially announced to his room-mate after putting finishing touches to his packing.

"You can't be serious, Jarafi said, looking at his friend disapprovingly. "You are not ready."

"But I am," Andreya said, somewhat surprised. "I'm all packed. Or have I overlooked something?"

"You mean you're going to try to win a girl dressed like that in a T-shirt? Oh, come on, Andreya, you need a decent shirt – and a neck tie!"

"Are you joking, Jarafi! A neck tie? Why, anyone can tell it'll be hot and sticky in the bus! Besides, I don't think I need to dress up for it. If I win Sekani at all, let it be me, and not my clothes."

"Sounds like good thinking," Jarafi said, nodding reflectively. Then he sprang to his feet, setting squeaking the old springs of the bed on which he had been sitting. He picked up Andreya's suitcase and led the way out.

When they reached one of the buses, Jarafi climbed up its ladder with Andreya's suitcase and wedged it among the other cases on the luggage rack. Then he and Andreya stepped into the nearly full bus. After some looking around, Jarafi spotted Eva towards the back of vehicle, sitting on the aisle end of a two-people seat she was sharing with Sekani. They walked straight to the two girls.

Eva rose, smiled at Andreya and, curtseying jokingly, motioned him to the space she had just vacated beside Sekani. "Reserved for you, Mr. Soko," she said, imitating the courtesy of an air hostess.

"You're not going by this bus then, Miss Midaya?" Andreya asked, addressing Eva with equal mock courtesy while his lips twitched with amusement as the trick dawned on him.

Jarafi answered for Eva: "Don't you know, Mr. Soko, that she comes from Gwembe district?" he said, identifying himself with the game of formality. "What would she be doing on a North- bound bus?"

"I see," Andreya said. He bowed toward Jarafi and said: "Then I take it she'll be on the same bus with you, Mr. Tauzi?"

Jarafi nodded, grinning.

"Well, thank you, Miss Midaya for the seat," Andreya said, bowing to Eva.

"My pleasure, Mr. Soko" she said, genuflecting exaggeratedly.

While all this joking around was going on, Sekani was looking out of the window, as if unaware of it all.

"Hi, Miss Zuza!" Andreya said, smilingly as he sat beside her on the seat.

"Hi, Mr Soko!" she returned with a giggle.

The four wished one another happy holidays and then Jarafi and Eva left the bus, stopping at the door to wave good-bye.

For one or two minutes after Jarafi and Eva had left the bus, Andreya and Sekani sat without saying a word to each other. But if Andreya didn't make use of his mouth, he certainly made use of his eyes, or rather his good eye. He noticed that around her red-and-white floral dress Sekani had wrapped a waist-to-ankle *chitenje* printed in the green and red national colours of the Republic of Dziko. He couldn't see much of the cloth, though; for sitting on Sekani's lap was a split-bamboo hand basket. From under a green doily that was daintily draped over the contents of the basket issued a line of green wool which she was deftly crocheting into another doily. Green seemed to be Sekani's favourite colour; for she was also wearing a loose-fitting, unbuttoned green cardigan, its long sleeves casually pushed up and gathered about the elbows. And loosely wrapped round her head was a brightly coloured but predominantly green *duku*.

11

Andreya thought the way the duku completely covered her ears, and the way it came down as far as her eye brows made her breath-takingly attractive.

"Hi, Sekani!" Andreya said, looking at her with a wide smile.

She looked up at him, smiling knowingly. "Well, hi again, Mr Soko!" she said. Her dimples, her soft, unhurried and somewhat lispy voice, and the way her full, moist lips curled when she spoke, warmed Andreya's heart.

"Oh, come off it, Sekani! That 'Mr.-Miss' game is gone with Jarafi and Eva!"

"Why should it?" Sekani asked in what was clearly mock protest. "Isn't it courteous to address one another by surnames?" A smile played around the corners of her mouth as she continued her crocheting.

Wasn't it courteous to address one another by surnames? Andreya was thrilled by the challenge to debate that question. They had got off to a good start, he thought. He recalled that Eva had said it shouldn't be difficult for him; and he wondered if he and Sekani had all along been mutual secret admirers.

CHAPTER THREE

The bus station in Bongwe town was a milling mass of travelers waiting for buses – a throng that neither increased nor decreased in size as packed out-going buses crossed ways with packed in-coming ones. Public travel was difficult at times like this, when colleges and schools closed at the same time.

At 6:30 p.m. Andreya and Sekani returned to the bus station from the restaurant where they had gone to eat. They had taken their time at the restaurant, thinking that the earliest the Vukula bus would arrive at the station from the depot was 6:30 p.m., half an hour before its scheduled departure time. And even that punctuality was unlikely at this time of peak demand for public transport: a time when buses could be hours behind their schedules. But when they reached the station, they found that the Vukula bus had arrived from the depot and was already surrounded by a crowd about twice its capacity: a noisy rabble of people jostling and shoving as they battled to get in.

Congratulating themselves for having had the good sense to buy their tickets immediately they had arrived in town by hired bus from Ginezi College that afternoon, Andreya and Sekani hurriedly carried their suitcases from the station's luggage store room to the bus. While Sekani stood by the cases, waiting to hand them up to the bus company's luggage assistant (who was already on the vehicle's ladder, busy putting passenger's luggage on the roof rack), Andreya plunged into the jostling rabble and fought his way into the bus.

Nearly every seat had been taken. Andreya went almost all the way to the back of the bus before he found an empty three-people seat. He leaned out of the window by the seat and called Sekani, who was still outside. She came over to the window and held up to him his briefcase and then her basket.

Turning to put Sekani's basket on the seat, Andreya was rather unpleasantly surprised to see Harold Mphande sitting in a drunken slouch at the other end of the seat. He quickly looked around. All seats had been taken. He must make the best of a bad situation: He must separate Harold and Sekani.

"Hi, Harold!" he said in feigned joy as he patted the befuddled fellow on the shoulder. "Would you like a window seat?"

"Been looking for one," Harold spluttered as he tottered to his feet. Andreya placed Sekani's basket in the centre of the seat and stepped into the aisle so as to let Harold pass. No sooner had Harold flopped onto the window end of the seat than he fell fast asleep. Andreya lifted Sekani's basket, placed it at the other end of the seat, and then sat down between it and Harold.

When Sekani finally got onto the bus and picked her way through the thick line of standing passengers to where Andreya had saved her a seat, she couldn't help laughing at the sight of a drink-stupefied Harold. Her shoulders rocked with suppressed laughter, causing Andreya to dread what might happen should Harold wake up to find her laughing at him. But Harold, his head slumped on his chest, snored away as though he were in his bedroom. His white shirt, unbuttoned and soiled with Bongwe town's red dust, hung loose and rumpled outside his tight-fitting corduroy trousers. His red neck tie was so extensively loosened it looked like a strip of old cloth carelessly knotted into a loop and then thrown round his neck.

"He didn't come on our bus, did he?" Sekani asked in a whisper as she wiped laughter tears.

"We'd have seen him," Andreya said. "He must have come on the other bus."

*   *   *

14

Crammed with its human load, the north-bound Vukula bus steadily crept its way through the moonless night. The general chit-chat among the passengers gradually died down and heads began to nod to the droning of the engine and the rattling of the ancient vehicle's window panes.

Around one o'clock in the morning, the bus pulled up at Fungo town, half-way between Bongwe and Vukula. Here a good number of people alighted, so that most of the passengers travelling further north who had been standing all the way form Bongwe now settled down onto seats. Outside, more people jostled in a line that had begun forming alongside the bus long before it came to a complete stop. The line extended from the door of the vehicle to well beyond its tail.

At Fungo, Harold stirred out of his sleep for the first time since Bongwe.

"Excuse me," he said to Andreya, gesturing with one hand his request for space to pass, and with the other rubbing his eyes sleepily.

"Are you dropping here, Mr. Mphande?" Andreya asked, hoping for a yes.

"No," came the coarse, sleepy reply. "I'm not dropping. I just want to go out for a while – to irrigate the roadside vegetation."

Andreya turned towards Sekani and, both of them smiling in grim humour at Harold's choice of words, they swung their knees to the right to make room for him to pass.

But instead of rising upon being given way, Harold grinned at Sekani, whom he had just noticed for the first time.

"Hey, Sekani baby!" he exclaimed, reaching across Andreya's lap to pat her on the arm. "You're going to Katoto, huh?"

"No," Sekani replied, jerking away from his hand. "I'm getting off at Mwera."

"Good enough, baby!" Harold spluttered. "We've enough time to chat between here and Mwera.... Let me pass.... When I come back, I'll sit beside you, baby. Then we'll chat and chat and chat. O.K.?"

Outside by the door, the conductor's ticket machine whirred away.

Coins chinked as the conductor counted cash and made change. One by one, new passengers stumbled aboard, some tremulously slipping the precious blue tickets into the safety of their purses or the folds of their dukus.

"I'm first taking those going all the way to Vukula!" the conductor shouted above the din. But the announcement only had the effect of causing the line to completely disintegrate. The crowd surged round the conductor and scores of cash-clutching hands jutted out before him, pushing one another out of the way as their owners loudly demanded tickets. It seemed everyone was bound for Vukula.

"Line, please!" the conductor yelled in vain as the throng swarmed over him. Pushed from behind, a young man who had been standing close to the conductor came crashing into him, causing the conductor to stagger backwards, thereby clearing the doorway, where he had been standing guard. With the door cleared, sheer strength was now the ticket with which to board the bus. It seemed the vehicle was going to topple over under the pressure of pushing and squeezing at the door.

Ruthlessly battered in the scramble, babies strapped on their mothers' backs screamed with discomfort. Their mothers, intent upon boarding the bus, puffed and wrenched their way through the hustle and jostle, apparently unmindful of their little ones' discomfort.

"'Line! Line!' – what for?" sneered a small old man as he triumphantly stepped aboard, his thin lips quivering from the tension he had undergone squeezing his way through the crush at the door. "I was not going to spend another night here! Buses have been leaving me since the day before yesterday!"

When the little man saw Andreya and Sekani sitting by themselves on a three-people seat, he purposefully advanced towards the seat, elbowing his way through the dense line of standing passengers.

"How can you two have a three-people seat all to yourselves?" he asked Andreya morosely.

"There are three of us on this seat, *bambo*," Andreya replied politely. "Our friend went out to relieve himself."

"He will have to stand this time," the little man said, his face serious. "Move over so I can sit down!" He gestured his stern order with a sweep of his arm. Andreya found the gesture grimly amusing: The little man's slim arm was swamped by the voluminous sleeve of an overcoat that had once been white, an oversize smoke-scented affair that trailed almost to the floor.

"He's drunk, *bambo*," Andreya told the little fellow. "He can't stand too well."

"That is his problem!" the little man yelled. "I say move and give me room on the seat!"

"But *bambo*, there are already three of us on this seat," Andreya insisted.

"Hey, child," the slight fellow said with a snort, leaning over and wagging a menacing finger at Andreya. "Do you know whom you are trying to argue with? Just move over and save yourself a lot of trouble."

"Move over, Andreya," Sekani said in a low voice.

"O.K.," Andreya said to her. "But we'd better have him occupy Harold's place. That way we'll save ourselves a lot of trouble! Let him pass."

"No, Andreya," Sekani said, as if struck by a sudden thought. "Let's have him sit where I'm sitting, and I'll sit where Harold sat. Remember what Harold said before going out?" She looked at Andreya meaningly.

Andreya smiled understandingly as he let her pass.

The little man sat down beside Andreya. Looking straight ahead and speaking much more loudly than was necessary, he said: "You school children act as if buses belong to your mothers. Remember, we all pay to board these buses. Besides, it is you school children who fill up buses, causing other travelers to wait days and days before they can catch a bus. Psss-haw!" he shot out his thin lips and sucked his teeth in disgust.

Andreya felt like telling him: 'It's all right now, old fellow. We no longer resent your company; in fact, we appreciate it now!'

People were still trying to get on the bus when it finally pulled out of Fungo and resumed its northward journey. At first Andreya wondered if Harold had been left behind. But several kilometers out of Fungo, he heard his drunken voice above the rumbling of the engine: He was somewhere up front, demanding to be given way to go to his seat at the back. The other standing passengers, who were so jammed they were stepping on one another's toes, were shouting him down, telling him that all the seats at the back were fully occupied.

After Fungo the bus didn't stop until it reached Mwera town at five a.m. The bus station here was only a few hundred metres from Mwera Primary School, where Sekani's aunt was a teacher.

"Are you getting off here, *bambo*?" a standing passenger asked Andreya when the latter took Sekani's basket and stood up.

"She is," Andreya replied, indicating Sekani. "I'm coming back; I'm only seeing her off the bus."

"May I join you?" the standing passenger asked, almost begged, gesturing to the seat. He looked very tired, having stood all the way from Bongwe.

"Oh sure," Andreya replied after dismissing the thought that Harold might still be interested in the seat. "As I said, I'm coming back. So please save my place."

Andreya led the way through the crammed line of standing passengers. They found Harold, now somewhat sober, standing about halfway up the aisle.

"Are you also dropping here?" Harold asked Andreya in a coarse but no longer drunken voice. His eyes quickly shifted from Andreya's face to Sekani's basket which Andreya was carrying. They were fixed on the basket as Andreya replied:

"No, I'm only seeing her off."

"I see," Harold said with a grin. Then he looked off toward the rear of the bus. "Hey, who's sitting in my place?" he asked rather indifferently.

"Some old fellow," Andreya told him. "I tried to stop him, but he was too stubborn. And the other man asked to join us when he saw that Sekani was getting off. I did think of saving your place, but the man looked so tired I couldn't decently say no to him."

"I'm no longer interested in the seat, anyway," Harold said morosely, still looking off, and mumbling the words as though he were thinking aloud.

"Bye, Harold!" Sekani said as she and Andreya resumed moving toward the door. "Happy holidays!"

"Yeah, you too," Harold mumbled, still looking away from the two of them.

CHAPTER FOUR

The bus reached Vukula town at ten o'clock that morning, five hours behind schedule. As it sped down the gravel main street of the town, it raised a cloud of swirling dust which the Asian shops that lined the windward side of the street took in through their open doors and windows. The townfolk, moving up and down from shop to shop, readily recognized it as the Bongwe-Vukula bus. They looked at their watches (others at the sun, which was half-way up the eastern sky) and wondered why the bus was so far behind schedule that day.

As the bus turned a bend in the street and the station came into view, one of the passengers cried out: "Look! The Chisika bus hasn't left yet! There it is!" As a result of this announcement, a small commotion arose among the passengers as nearly half of them began to make themselves ready for a quick get-off as soon as their bus would come to a stop. They could see that the Chisika bus, parked in front of the cream-and-green station building, was already full. There was only standing room on it.

The in-coming bus had hardly come to a stop when Andreya looked out of the window and saw Harold Mphande dash for the ticket window, weaving through the teeming crowds of travelers and leaping over a profusion of suitcases, baskets and bags. In a few moments he was back to the bus that had just brought him. He climbed the vehicle's ladder and brought down his suitcase from the luggage rack. Staggering with the weight of the case, he ran to the Chisika bus, found someone to help him take up his luggage to the vehicle's roof rack, and then boarded the bus. He accomplished all this while many of those who also wanted to catch the Chisika bus were still trying to get off the Bongwe-Vukula bus.

The Chisika bus had long left when Andreya stepped off the bus that had just brought him. He felt relieved to be rid of Harold. He thought: 'The poor fellow is jealous of me over Sekani. Too bad for him: He has two more terms before he completes his training. For two long terms he'll eat his heart out over us!

For Andreya was quite certain he had won Sekani. Their chat from Ginezi College till she alighted at Mwera had left him with no doubt as to her affection for him. He recalled the sweet bashful look in her eyes whenever he had steered the conversation to the romantic side. On such occasions she would lift a corner of her green cardigan to her mouth and nibble at it. That was always a good sign: It was common knowledge among the young men that when a girl engages in such bashful actions she is communicating a positive message to her suitor. In this connection, Andreya would always remember an incident several years back. He and his friend Jonazi had been sent on an errand to Mwazisi Mission, some thirty kilometres from their home area. They had borrowed bicycles for the trip.

After crossing the Lusiba river, which was less than half a kilometer from the mission station, they met a girl who was returning from shopping at Mwazisi. Jonazi liked her at once. So they stopped her and began to chat with her.

The girl was standing beside a mtanthanyerere bush that was about her height. No sooner had the chatting started than she began plucking the leaves of the bush. Then she started breaking off the fronds... then the twigs... then whole branches. By the end of the chat – which lasted more than an hour – she had ripped a good many branches off the bush.

After the two young men had at last released the girl, Jonazi said, "She is now mine, Andreya." He turned to take one more look at her as she swayed gracefully down the slope.

"What makes you think that?" Andreya asked sceptically "She was quite difficult; and, as far as I can remember, she did not give you any definite answer."

"The bush," Jonazi said. "You saw how she ripped it down in her bashfulness. That is how I can tell!" They laughed as they adjusted the pedals and then mounted their bicycles.

Sure enough, after Jonazi and Andreya had later on paid the girl a visit at her home, marriage negotiations commenced. Before long Jonazi's parents took care of the bride price and he and the girl were married.

Stepping down now from the Bongwe-Vukula bus, Andreya smiled at the thought that Jonazi occasionally teased his wife about the mtanthanyerere bush on the road to Mwazisi.

Andreya learnt that his bus, the Katoto bus, hadn't left yet. It was still in the depot behind the station building, undergoing some repairs. The bus, whose normal departure time was eight a.m., had now been delayed by over two hours.

It was close on noon when Andreya's bus finally rumbled out of Vukula and headed north for Katoto town. Three hours later it pulled up at Monire bus stop and a dust-covered Andreya alighted. He picked up his suitcase, which was laden mainly with books, hoisted it onto his shoulder, and began the trek to Mbuyeni, his home area, seven difficult kilometres to the east of the road.

*   *   *

The sandy track lay monotonously straight before Andreya. He was now only about two kilometres from his village. To his left, running parallel to the track, was Karizga dambo. In the rainy season, Karizga was a swampy march that bred millions of croaking frogs and trilling crickets. But, since the first rains hadn't come yet (they were unusually late that year, for normally they came towards the end of November), Karizga was still as parched and black as the dry-season bush fires had left it. A maze of cracked trails criss-crossed the blackened dambo; they were paths worn by the neighbourhood folk as they daily crossed Karizga to gather masuku, the fruit which at that time of year dropped from musuku trees abounding on the banks of the dambo.

Stopping by a musuku tree whose fruit he knew to be more delicious than that of most musuku trees around, Andreya hoisted his suitcase off his shoulder and put it down at the edge of the track. He walked over to the musuku tree, which stood in a clump of other trees a couple of metres off the track.

"Someone has been here already," he said to himself after looking around the tree and seeing nothing but a profusion of the broad dry musuku leaves covering the ground. However, by walking around the tree and looking more closely among the leaves, he managed to gather a handful of the golden-brown fruits. One after another he pressed the lusciously ripe fruits between his forefinger and thumb, cracking their delicate skin. Holding the cracked section of the fruit to his mouth, he sucked out the yellow flesh, the delicious juice, and the flesh-covered pips. He rolled the pips around in his mouth for a while before spitting them out.

Suddenly, a song broke the late-afternoon quiet, interrupting his snack. Through the tangled leafless twigs of the clump, Andreya peered in the direction of the singing. About a hundred metres further down Karizga, four boys were performing a sort of circle dance in the centre of the dambo. Three of them were each dragging behind them a leafy katope branch. Andreya recognized the fourth boy, who was taller and thinner than the others (and the oldest), as his half-brother Lunya. Circling around with the other boys, Lunya held a bow, arrow already fitted.

Andreya smiled at the old method of stalking a sitting nightjar. The song – meaningless words sung to a hunting tune – and the sound of the leafy katope branches being dragged on the ground, were believed to have the effect of hypnotizing the bird. As he watched the scene before him, a surge of nostalgia for his own long-lost boyhood welled up within him.

After the boys had danced round the nightjar a few times, Lunya stopped behind the wide-awake night bird and drew the cord of his bow. While he took aim, the other boys continued to drag their branches round the bird, singing with mounting excitement.

Then Lunya released the arrow, and it flew straight at the nightjar.

"*Atchii!*" he let out the cry which among all hunters in that area, boys and men alike, meant 'I got it.'

The poor bird took off, lamely fluttering its wings.

"I broke its wing!" Lunya shrieked excitedly as he snatched up the arrow he had used. "Did you see how awkwardly it flew off?" Frantically, he selected a fresh arrow from a collection of five he clasped against his bow. He fitted it and dashed for a small ant mound about fifty metres away near which he had seen the bird land.

His companions abandoned their branches, picked up their bows and, their arrows fitted, ran after him.

He stopped within a few metres of the ant mound and signalled halt to his friends by holding out his right hand, palm open, behind him. While he was giving the signal, his keen eyes were searching the area around the ant nest. Within seconds he spotted the well camouflaged grayish-brown bird. Then he cautiously raised his bow, drew the cord, and took aim. But just as he was about to release the arrow, the wounded bird took wing. This time, however, it didn't go very far. After a few limp flaps of its wings, it landed awkwardly about ten metres from him.

"*Hlomo!* (I go shares)" shouted one of the other boys, who, having out-run the others, was near enough to see that the poor bird didn't have half a chance of escaping with its life.

Lunya chased after his quarry. But the wounded bird, unwilling to die without a struggle, kept taking off each time he raised his bow to shoot. However, as the chase became hotter, the distances between the bird's landings became shorter and shorter. Eventually the disabled bird plunged into the thicket from where Andreya was watching the whole chase. It landed about a metre from him and he pounced on it.

Hiding the wide-headed and large-eyed bird behind him, its short, hook-billed mouth wide open as it gasped for breath, Andreya stepped out of the clump.

"He akuru!" (Look, it's my brother)" Lunya exclaimed, bringing to an astonished stop his pursuit of the nightjar. For moments, he stood still, leaning on his bow as though it were a crutch. His big eyes, twinkling through a squinty, bashful smile, and his perfectly even teeth, their maize-grain whiteness emphasized by the soot-dark background of his face, radiated all the vitality and spiritedness of a seven-year-old.

"E, he akuru!" the other three boys chorused as they ran up to where Lunya and Andreya were standing.

When Lunya and the other boys offered their right hands in greeting, Andreya gave them his left, jokingly explaining that he had been hurt in the other hand. But when one boy stole a peek behind Andreya and, laughing, announced what he had seen, Andreya held out the nightjar before him.

"You're getting to be quite a hunter, Lunya," Andreya said, smiling at the youngster. "Which arrow did you use?"

"This one," Lunya said, extracting the arrow from the collection clasped against his bow.

Andreya looked admiringly at the expertly crafted weapon the boy held out before him. Its thin yet sturdy reed shaft was well trimmed and very straight. At one end of the shaft a notch for fitting the arrow to the bow's cord had been carved; and at the other end was fitted an artistically carved brown arrowhead of hard, old mphangala wood. Like the other four, the arrow measured about a metre from the cord notch to the thorn-sharp tip of the arrowhead.

"Had you drawn the cord with a little more strength," Andreya said to Lunya, "that fine arrow should have killed the bird right there over its eggs. Look, the tip didn't go deep enough...." He held out the nightjar and pointed to a spot covered with clotting blood on the bird's left shoulder.

Receiving the nightjar from Andreya, Lunya took a brief look at the spot where the tip of his arrowhead had shallowly pierced the bird. Then, suddenly looking up at Andreya, he smiled inquisitively and said: "So you've been watching us stalk the bird!"

Andreya grinned. "Yes," he said, "right from the start. I've been eating masuku over there."

As the boys looked in the direction Andreya was pointing, one of them saw Andreya's suitcase sitting at the edge of the track, its silver-plated locks glinting in the setting sun.

"Look!" the boy who had seen the suitcase exclaimed. "He has just arrived from college. He has not been to the village yet; there is his suitcase. I will carry it home!" He dashed for the case.

"No, I will carry it!" two other boys protested in one breath and gave chase.

"None of them can carry that heavy suitcase," Andreya told Lunya, laughing towards the racing boys. Then he put his arm round the youngster's shoulders and turned him around, motioning him to lead the way to the suitcase.

"Did you have a good journey?" Lunya asked, wringing the nightjar's neck as he walked along ahead of Andreya.

"A very good journey," Andreya replied. "But had the Katoto bus gone according to its normal schedule, I'd have missed it. The bus I took at Bongwe last night was so slow on the way that we reached Vukula when the sun was this high...." For the benefit of the Standard One youngster, who had not yet been taught to read time, Andreya pointed with his palm half-way up the eastern sky. "But when we reached Vukula I was lucky to find that the Katoto bus, which normally leaves Vukula at sunrise, had not yet left; they were repairing it."

When Andreya and Lunya reached the suitcase, Andreya laughed to see the three boys, who had so enthusiastically raced one another to get to the suitcase first, standing defeated around it.

"Well, strong men," Andreya said between gasps of laughter. "Who's going to carry the suitcase?"

"*Eeee,* it's heavy!" the three boys chorused shrilly.

"Even Lunya, he cannot so much as lift it!" said Buti, the youngest, with a giggle.

"Say 'a-Lunya', silly!" one boy, named Thinkhu, reprimanded the little one stiffly. "Don't you know that a-Lunya is the oldest of us all? When are you going to learn to mention the names of your seniors with respect?"

"A-Lunya," Buti corrected himself, timidly burrowing a small foot in and out of the sand.

"He has no ears, this naughty child," another boy, Muloyiso, chided the offender. "Only this morning, a-Thinkhu slapped him on the cheek for mentioning his name without respect. Did you not slap him, a-Thinkhu?" He looked up at Thinkhu as if pleading for a yes.

· "I do not fool around with cheeky rascals, myself," Thinkhu said with great airs. "The next time he repeats what he did this morning, I'll slap him in front of his mother." Actually, the boy didn't use the word for 'slap'. Instead, he used an angry variation of it coined on the spur of the moment: a word whose very sound conveyed the viciousness with which the slap would be administered.

"All right, all right, my friends," intervened Andreya, who had been listening to the youngsters' exchanges with a condescending smile. "Time to go. Don't you worry: I'll carry my old suitcase. Come on, Buti; you lead the way."

The boys trooped in silence ahead of Andreya, raising a low film of white dust from the sandy track. Although darkness was slowly gathering around them, they could see that the top half of a ridge of hills about five kilometers ahead of them was still bathed in the golden glow of sunset. This sunlight that lingered on the hilltops while dusk settled on the plains below was locally called *mhanya wa bachimbwi* (hyenas' sunlight); for it was believed that hyenas came out of their caves and basked in this soft sunlight before starting their nightly raids on the neighbourhood villages.

Walking along behind the boys, Andreya was lost in thought as he now looked at his half-brother Lunya, who was immediately in front of him. Somehow, looking at Lunya padding along with the other boys reminded him that he, his two younger half-brothers (Lunya and his elder brother Phyoka), his father Kaneli and step-mother Nyasato were strangers in Mbuyeni. And that thought in turn set him thinking about what he had been told by his father concerning the developments that had led to their being banished from Nchena, their original home area....

Andreya's mother – Nyasato the elder – had died of a birth complication while delivering her first child (Andreya himself). Because Kaneli's parents-in-law had liked him so much, they had offered him the deceased's younger sister as *mbirigha*, a sort of replacement for his late wife. And so, as both Kaneli and Nyasato the younger were Christians and both agreed to be husband and wife, they were duly married in the Church.

Not long after Kaneli's second wedding, however, his beloved parents-in-law were struck dead by lightning while they were planting groundnuts in a field near their village. Suspecting that the bolt was an act of witchcraft, Jozeni, the late couple's only son among their three children, went to consult a famous witchdoctor, Dekhani, who told him that the lightning had indeed been a spell, cast by none other than Kaneli. Dekhani added that Kaneli had also taught his new wife the mysterious art of witchery.

After that there had been no peace in Kaneli's family. Jozeni not only threatened revenge, but also attempted to force Nyasato to leave Kaneli. Nyasato, however, wouldn't let anyone part them. This made Jozeni so angry that he disowned her, swearing never to call her his sister again, and never to allow her and her children to set foot in his home.

Kaneli had also been in trouble in his own village. On the strength of the witchcraft accusations leveled against his son, Kaneli's father – in his capacity as Village Headman Khuyo – was advised by his counselors to force Kaneli and Nyasato to go to Dekhani and be cleansed. But, in obedience to the dictates of their Christian faith (and in any case, as far as they were concerned, Dekhani was a lying mischief-maker), Kaneli and Nyasato refused to go to the witchdoctor.

Consequently the village headman reluctantly yielded to pressure from his counselors and banished Kaneli and his family from Nchena. He sent them some two hundred kilometres away to Mbuyeni, the area of Village Headman Mbavi, a friend of his, whom he asked to kindly give them land on which to build.

Kaneli had harboured no grudge against his father for banishing him from his home area; he knew he had done it due to tremendous pressure from his advisors. And when the old man later died of old age, Kaneli went to Nchena to bury him. Yet when, shortly afterwards, Kaneli's mother was fatally bitten by a poisonous snake, people in Nchena accused him of having caused not only her death but also that of his father.

Despite the loss of both his parents, Kaneli had felt he still had a father in Village Headman Mbavi. So when the latter had also passed away only five years after the arrival of Kaneli and his family in Mbuyeni, Kaneli grieved as much as he had grieved at his own father's death. For Mbavi had been very kind to him and his family. And during his reign, no one in Mbuyeni had dared gossip that Kaneli was a wizard. As a result, no sooner had they settled in Mbuyeni than the circumstances that had led to their presence there were forgotten.

But after Village Headman Mbavi had passed away, malicious. gossip and rumours against Kaneli's family revived. The succeeding village headman was either powerless or simply unwilling to put a stop to them.

And the rumours had intensified when Andreya passed the Primary Leaving Examination and went to secondary school. The fact that he was the only one the Ministry of Education had selected for secondary education out of all the pupils who had passed the examination at Mbuyeni Primary School did not help matters:

– "See? Those people's charms are so powerful they can influence even the Government!"

– "During the exam, I noticed that Andreya was wearing something around his wrist. That must have been an exam amulet."

– "You will see: That boy will go straight to the university after secondary school."

Andreya had not gone to the university, though. Instead, the Ministry of Education had selected him for Ginezi Teacher Training College, a government-run college for training primary school teachers. When Dziko was still under colonial rule, Ginezi College had been a most sough-after college. The very name Ginezi was then quite a trade mark in the teaching profession; any teacher who had "finished at Ginezi" was held in high regard. But since attaining independence in 1964, the young Republic of Dziko had made great strides in education as well as in other fields. During those few years of self-determination, a university had been built; several primary school teacher training colleges had been added to those already in existence; and hundreds of secondary schools had sprung up all over the young nation. The result was that Ginezi lost its original aura of greatness and charm, becoming simply one of the country's several primary school teacher training colleges. To be selected for Ginezi College was thus no longer an enviable thing. Now secondary school students were competing for admission to the country's only university….

Suddenly, Andreya realized that something was going on among the boys trooping along ahead of him in the white dust of the sandy track – something which called for his immediate intervention. Muloyiso had resumed the attack on young Buti's lack of respect for his seniors. He, Muloyso, had cited another past occasion when Buti had mentioned Thinkhu's name disrespectfully. The boys had enthusiastically taken up the matter and begun to scold Buti.

"How's your father, Buti?" Andreya asked as a way of intervening into the explosive situation among the boys.

"He's well," little Buti answered in a subdued voice.

"Has he woven many split-bamboo baskets lately?" Andreya pursued, determined to have the boys forget their quarrel with Buti altogether.

Lunya answered for Buti: "A-Guza has woven very many split-bamboo baskets lately. This afternoon I saw him tying to a pole various sizes of baskets. He said he was preparing to carry them to Fule tomorrow."

So Guza was going to sell baskets at Fule tomorrow! How fortunate for Andreya! For he had decided to write Sekani right away, and had been wondering how he could get the letter to Fule Post Office – the nearest post office at about ten kilometers from Mbuyeni – as soon as possible. During the seven-kilometre walk from Monire bus stop, he had not only thought out what he was going to say in his first letter to her, but had actually mentally composed the entire letter. He would write it tonight and Guza would post it for him at Fule tomorrow.

CHAPTER FIVE

The long-overdue rains finally came, drenching Mbuyeni and filling its streams – hitherto dry, thirsty strips of white sand – with that most precious among nature's gifts: water. The maize fields, which had long been made ready, were immediately planted with maize, beans, pumpkins and cow peas – all in one field. Millet was sown in separate, newly opened patches .... For those who loved to work the soil, the rainy season always came as a welcome change from the drudgery of the dry season.

The period between planting and weeding was a comparatively restful interlude in the growing season. The maize fields did not look green yet, since all they had in them were tender shoots of the plants that had just nosed out of the soil. In a few days the shoots would unfold into leaves, and weeding would then commence. In the meantime, as they waited for their maize field to be ready for weeding, the people of Mbuyeni tilled separate plots of land in which they planted groundnuts. But since groundnuts were not treated with as much respect as maize (the staple crop), the groundnut patches were invariably much smaller than the maize plots. In fact, although groundnuts had great cash value (they could be sold to the Government at a much higher price that any of the other crops), the man was considered a fool who had so large a groundnut plot that it prevented him from giving due attention to his maize fields.

Thus the few days between planting and weeding formed the least busy period of the entire growing season. Whereas during the long weeding period people would go out into the fields long before sunrise and trudge back to the village at dusk, during this intermediate period the groundnut plots didn't keep the villagers away from home all day. By mid-afternoon most people would be back in the village. The men would then lounge in the cool of their verandas, while the tireless women would make a smooth change from field work to their endless household chores.

One hot afternoon during this period, Andreya's father, Keneli Soko, was resting in the shade of his veranda after the morning's work in his groundnut patch. He was chatting with a neighbour, who was also lounging on his veranda a few metres across the village compound.

"The rains came beautifully this year, did they not, a-Mchona?" Kaneli's deep, confident voice boomed across the compound to the other man. "Although they came late, that first deluge really soaked the earth. And the light rains – interspersed with sunny spells – which we've been getting for the past few days have caused our seeds to germinate well."

"You should see our maize field over at Sinda, Soko," Mchona said with the delight a conversation about crops never fails to bring out in a farmer. "Every single seed we sowed has germinated."

"I know, I know," Kaneli said with equal delight. "I passed through the field earlier this afternoon. If the rains continue in this manner, you should have an excellent yield from that field this year."

"There's every sign that the rains will continue falling this way, Soko," Mchona said, a ring of certainty in his voice. "Look: yesterday it rained. Today we have had a sunny, warm day. And those clouds rising on the horizon yonder indicate it will rain tomorrow. And the day after tomorrow – a nice warm day. And so on. Haaa, we are going to have a good season, Soko!"

"Yes …. Oh, by the way, I had great luck passing through your field at Sinda this afternoon. On that anthill near the upper end of the field, I found three very large *utali* mushrooms. You should have seen their stems – so big and so long!"

"That is another sign that we shall have a good harvest this year," Mchona said with a triumphant sweep of his hand. "I cannot remember when last we had such an abundant spawning of the *utali* mushroom...."

By sunset that day, all the men in the village had gathered outside Village Headman Mbavi's mphala. This was a round hut in which the three-wived chief lived alone as though he were a widower. Every evening in the rainy season all the men in the village gathered in the mphala for fellowship. Also the mphala was the only acceptable eating place for men. A man who ate alone in his own house was not only condemned as selfish, but also ridiculed as effeminate. Women prepared the food in their respective houses and then had the little boys carry it to the mphala.

These evening mphala gatherings were almost always initiated by Kaneli; and that day was no exception. He had walked over to the mphala and sat leaning against the sunset side of the hut, soaking in the warmth of the setting sun as he carved a new handle for his hoe. One by one the other men had joined him, some leaning against the sun-warmed wall, others pulling up logs that happened to be lying around, and sitting on them. Most of the men were working on hoe or axe handles, carving or smoothing them with their razor-sharp axes. The single topic of conversation was farm work.

When Village Headman Mbavi emerged from the house of one of his three wives and walked over to where the men were gathered, Andreya, who was smoothing a new axe handle, rose and walked toward the door of the mphala.

"You are joining us out here, are you not, *basekuru*?" he asked the village chief, calling him grandfather. "I will bring your goatskin."

"Thank you, my grandchild," said the old man. "It is a nice, warm evening, and the ground is dry. Who would want to be indoors as long as it is still light outside?"

"Lunya!" Nyasato's voice wafted to the mphala through the still evening air. She was calling from her kitchen hut.

34

Andreya knew what his step-mother was calling his half-brother for. So he put down the axe handle he was working on and started for Nyasato's kitchen.

"Lunyaaa!" Nyasato was calling impatiently now.

"He's not back from looking for mushrooms!" Andreya called back to his mother as he walked toward her kitchen.

"Ah, but these boys!" Nyasato complained out-loud as if addressing the whole village. "What sort of looking for mushrooms is this? ... You should not be carrying food to the mphala when young ones are around, Andreya. Where is Phyoka?"

"I sent him to the grocery."

As he carried the *sima* to the mphala, Andreya's heart leapt when he imagined Phyoka bringing a letter from Sekani. For what he had told his mother about having sent Phyoka to the grocery was only half true. He had indeed given Phyoka an empty coca-cola bottle, asking him to buy some paraffin at Matchipisa grocery, which was only a few metres from Mbuyeni Primary School – the initial destination of Phyoka's errand. Andreya had sent his 10-year-old half-brother on the errand to check at the headmaster's house if someone had brought some mail from Fule. Three weeks had gone by since his first letter to Sekani had been posted. He had been expecting a reply from her for a week now.

Andreya stopped in front of the door of the mphala. "Should I put the sima inside?" he asked the men.

"No, bring it here," several voices replied.

Andreya set down the dish of sima before the village headman and then ran back to his mother's kitchen to bring the relish and the water.

The sima filled the oval tin bowl generously. A matching bowl covered the mound of the maize mash – or, more correctly, hung high on it so that several centimetres of the white lump were exposed between the rims of the two bowls.

Village Headman Mbavi looked at the steaming dish before him, swallowed audibly, and said: "Nyasato beats most women in this village on the size of sima they send to the mphala. Many of them use very small bowls, which they do not even fill with sima. Do they not realize that we have to leave a quarter of every lump of sima for the boys? Pss-haw!" He pouted and sucked his teeth as he shook his grey head disapprovingly. "I suggest," he went on, "that each one of us should buy his wife bowls as big as Nyasato's. And be sure to tell them to always fill them up with mphala sima!"

The other men burst into a roar of laughter at the headman's proposal.

"*Bamdala bakuneneska* (the old man is right)," Mchona said, coughing out the words in dying gasps of laughter. "Surely, what do we work hard in the fields for? To eat well, of course!"

"The way our women feed us in this village would make one think we are running out of grain," another man commented.

Mchona said: Nyasoto also beats them on the amount of relish sent to the *mphala*, say, what's the relish, Soko?"

"*Awee*! (pity me)" Kaneli lamented in his rich baritone. "Where can one find good relish at this time of year? I think she has cooked the *utali* mushrooms I found in your maize field at Sinda this afternoon."

Mchona began to taunt Kaneli: "My goodness, Soko! When are you going to treat us to some of those tender *viwunda?* You must have scores of them in those pigeon coops of yours. And you can't deny it – the whole village hears their shrill whistling. And each time I pass by those coops I see dozens of *viwunda* being fed by parent pigeons under the eaves of the coops." "And *viwunda* are particularly tasty at this time of year, Soko," another man observed with a chuckle.

After Andreya and the men had eaten their share of the sima, Andreya covered the bowls of leftover sima and relish and took them into the mphala. When he emerged from the hut, his heart thumped at the sight of Phyoka coming up the village compound. Behind him trooped Lunya and the other boys, each of them proudly carrying a long-stemmed utali mushroom.

Sure enough, Phyoka brought some mail. Three of the four letters he brought were from South Africa: Once in several months, sons of the village working in that country wrote to their wives or parents back home. The fourth letter was the one Andreya had been waiting for so anxiously.

"Boys, there is sima for you in the mphala," Andreya told the youngsters after Phyoka had given him the letter. Normally, Andreya would have joined the men in chiding the little ones for having been in the bush till dusk. But receiving that letter had made him kindly disposed, and so he spoke nicely to the youngsters. "And Phyoka, after you have eaten, make a fire in the mphala; it is getting dark outside." He was already running towards his hut to go and read the letter when he made the last statement.

Andreya didn't quite know what to think of Sekani's letter. He had written her a rather sentimental letter: And he had felt he had cause to do so, and to expect from her a reply that had some sentiment in it; for he felt that on that trip from college, the girl had only stopped short of declaring her love for him. But this letter did not betray any feelings for him on Sekani's part.

It was a long letter, full of news of what she had done since the day she arrived at her aunt's at Mwera. But that was all. He read it four times that evening, and he read it over and over again during the remaining few days of the holidays, each time looking in vain for tell-tale choices of words. There were none.

The salutation of the letter didn't even have "dear" in it; it was simply "Andreya ..." And, most disconcerting of all, while he had ended his letter with "Much love, Andreya," Sekani's letter uncomittingly closed with "Sincerely, Sekani."

There was only one ray of hope in the letter: Andreya had in his letter asked her if she could wait for him at Mwera at the end of the holidays so that the two of them could travel back to college together. In her reply Sekani had agreed to the proposal without any reservations.

So, when the day for him to return to college arrived, Andreya walked the seven kilometres to Monire bus stop mildly thrilled by the resolve that before reaching Ginezi he will have solved the puzzle posed by Sekani's letter.

CHAPTER SIX

Ginezi College's driver Jumbe nudged Jarafi with his left knee and asked: "What's her name?"

Jumbe – a jovial old fellow dressed in a splendid-fitting khaki uniform – and Jarafi (who sat beside him in the cab of the college lorry) were bouncing along the quarter-kilometre gravel road that linked the college to the nearby MI road. They were on their way to the bus stop, where they were to wait for students returning to college from the country's northern and central provinces.

"Who?" Jarafi inquired, looking up at the elderly man.

"The young lady you're going to meet," the driver said, winking his left eye at Jarafi.

"Oh!" Jarafi said with a giggle. "It's not a young lady! It's my room-mate. You know Andreya Soko, don't you?"

"Oooh, *pepani!*" Jumbe apologised with a chuckle as he patted Jarafi on the thigh. "I thought it was – you know...." He gestured the female bust with his left hand. Then he said: "No, I don't believe I know your room-mate."

"Oh, I'm sure you know Andreya. Didn't you come to the two plays the Drama Club put on last term? That first year actor with a bad left eye."

Jumbe's face instantly became alive. "Oh, it's that one?" he exclaimed. "That young man amazes me. Where did he learn to act so well? And I hear he's a fine young man too – I mean as a person."

"One of the best I've known," Jarafi said, his voice full of great conviction. "He and I get along really well. It's a pity we're parting next term."

"By the way, this is your last year," Jumbe remarked

No sooner had Jumbe parked the lorry at the bus stop than a bus, its roof rack stacked high with suitcases, emerged on the skyline to their right. A few minutes later it was easing to a halt at the bus stop.

"There's your friend," Sekani said to Andreya, with whom she was sharing a seat on the bus.

"Oh yes, there's Jarafi!" Andreya said, rising to his feet – only to be roughly lurched against the back of the seat in front of him as the driver jammed on the brakes. Mumbling a brief apology to Sekani as he leaned past her to the window, he poked his head out. "Hi there, Jarafi!" he called out.

"Andreya!" Jarafi exclaimed, both his arms going up in greeting. "Welcome back!" He walked over to the side of the bus. "Whereabouts is your suitcase?"

"Right in the middle of the left side," Andreya told him, "And please bring down Sekani's as well. It's the green one next to mine, on the right."

"Of course," Jarafi said and winked at his pal. Then he turned and skipped to the bus's ladder.

"It went fine with Sekani, I take it?" Jarafi whispered to Andreya as the two walked toward the college lorry behind two younger students whose suitcases had been the last to be brought down from the roof rack by Jarafi. The rest of the students were already on the lorry.

"Yes," Andreya replied flatly.

Jarafi was surprised at his friend's unenthusiastic reply, which seemed to indicate that Andreya wasn't sure if it had gone fine with Sekani. Jarafi was all the more confused when they climbed aboard the lorry; for they found that Sekani had saved two places beside her on the wood-and-wrought-iron bench: for Andreya and for him. He watched the two closely during the ride to the college. But he still wasn't sure what to think when he jumped off the lorry at the roundabout in the centre of the quadrangle formed by the boy's dorms.

Indeed Andreya wasn't sure what to think either. In fact, for the rest of that term Sekani left him in utter confusion as to how she felt about him. The strange part of it was that he and Sekani saw more and more of each other as the term progressed. She never turned him down whenever he asked her out to various college activities and other occasions. In fact, the two were so much together that everybody in the college thought they were sweethearts. That is, everybody except Eva Midaya and Jarafi. These two knew for sure that Andreya and Sekani didn't have an affair between them.

Although Jarafi knew about Andreya's feelings for Sekani, Eva was in total darkness as to Sekani's innermost feelings for Andreya. Jarafi and Andreya discovered this when they once asked Eva if her inscrutable room-mate had told her anything that would suggest she was in love with Andreya. Eva told them that since the beginning of that term, Sekani had become very uncommunicative about her relationship with Andreya. She told them that once or twice the previous term, Sekani had freely confessed her fascination for Andreya. But these days, said Eva, Sekani talked very guardedly of him.

"The girl no longer loves you, Andreya," Jarafi told his room-mate one night. "At least it seems that way. If I were you, I'd start looking elsewhere.

"But I can't, Jarafi!" Andreya said emphatically. "I haven't felt for any girl the way I feel for Sekani; and I don't think I can love any other girl the way I love her. Each time I'm with her, I find that my love for her has grown deeper than before. Dozens of times I've bluntly confessed this to her. But her response has always been that she doesn't think she can commit herself as more than just a friend."

Jarafi said: "The funny thing about this entire relationship of yours is that she's so much attached to you that everybody thinks you two are lovers. It would make some sense if she had a lover somewhere; but she has indicated to Eva that she doesn't."

"It's a puzzle, Jarafi," Andreya said with a fascinated and confident chuckle. "But puzzles are there to be solved."

CHAPTER SEVEN

It was break time on a bright July morning towards the end of term at Ginezi College. Andreya was leaning against the wall of one of the red-brick classroom blocks, reading in the soft sunshine. He half-turned when he heard light footsteps behind him.

"Hi, Sekani!" he said, closing the book as he turned to face her.

"Hi, Andreya!" she returned, pronouncing the name with a lispy lilt that always thrilled Andreya. She was wearing his favourite pink cotton dress which she loosely topped with the inevitable green cardigan, ever unbuttoned, with its long sleeves casually gathered about the elbows.

Andreya was about to start telling her about the play he was reading in the book when he noticed that Sekani's face was rather troubled. Her big brown eyes looked anxious as she glanced round the little groups of two or three students absorbing the warm sun on the velvet crabgrass lawn.

"Read this, Andreya." She handed him a note, dropping as she did so a curtsey that bobbed the simple imitation silver ear rings which dangled from her pierced lobes. "Harold shoved it into my hand a few minutes ago."

"Harold?" Andreya said, receiving the folded piece of paper. He had barely managed to keep his voice calm, and his heart was already racing. A dull ache began to throb in his bad eye, where Harold had hit him the previous evening.

"Mmm," Sekani's affirmative mumble chocked in her throat. "I'm so sorry, Andreya, about what happened last night."

At Sekani's words of sympathy anger flashed up in Andreya's functioning eye. His broad brow furrowed slightly. "What senseless jealousy!" he said, his voice a bit louder than usual. "Anyhow, I was going to tell you about the whole sordid incident after class this afternoon. But I suppose I might as well tell –"

"Don't, Andreya," she said, interrupting him. "I think you'd better not tell me now; he makes some mad threats in that note. Let's wait until he's safely out of college. The second year students are leaving after lunch, anyway. You can tell me about it this afternoon."

"What does he say in here, anyway?" Andreya said. He bit his lower lip in anger as he began to unfold the piece of paper.

"Please, Andreya!" Sekani pleaded, placing her slim soft hand on his arm as she once again scanned the groups of students on the lawn. "Read it later – when you're alone. See you later!" With that, she turned and walked off the way she had come.

After watching her sway away gracefully until she had disappeared round the building, Andreya turned his attention to the note in his hand. Silently furious at Harold, he unfolded it.

The piece of paper had been roughly plucked out of an exercise book. On it had been scrawled:

Woman,

This is to warn you and your one-eyed lover that you'd better watch out these next few hours. Last night your idiot of a lover had the cheek to say I interfere with your monkey-business affair. Well, that earned him a sound beating from me. He must be grateful someone came to his rescue: I meant to deal with him pretty roughly! Now, just let me catch the two of you back-biting me during the next few hours and you gonna be sorry. I'm gonna squash that single eye of his and smash that watery head of yours. Keep out of my way, you nincompoops!

– They call me His Majesty Unworried Guy.

Andreya folded the piece of paper and put it in the inside pocket of his maroon college uniform blazer. He wiped the sweat that had been beading on his brow while he read the note. Then he turned and began to walk back to his classroom.

"'His Majesty'," Andreya scowled at Harold Mphande's self-styled title. Harold's over-enthusiastic admirers thought it was very clever the way he had come up with the title by adopting it from his initials. He might as well have titled himself 'His Madness', thought Andreya as he entered the classroom. He was warm all over, despite the coldness of the room.

That afternoon Andreya and Sekani went for a walk.

"Well, Sekani," Andreya said, his hands thrust in his blazer's pockets as he sauntered along beside her, looking straight ahead. "This is what happened last night...." Smiling wryly, he lowered his head and kicked a pebble along twice before looking ahead again. "Chiromba started it all," he continued. "He had come into our room and was chatting with Jarafi when, in that loud voice of his, he jokingly said to Jarafi: 'I'll be missing most of you guys. But there's one fellow whom I'll not in the least miss – the so-called His Majesty. I'm glad the rascal is leaving. He's been meddling with my girlfriend.'"

Andreya paused and looked at Sekani to see how she was taking it so far. But her eyes were fixed on the road as she walked along beside him.

"Well, the next thing we knew was that Harold had burst into the room," Andreya continued. "He went straight to my bed, where I lay relaxing, and began to accuse me of having said the words. Then he proceeded to shout all manner of insults and obscenities at me. When I sat up and tried to reason with him, he lunged at me. Our engagement was brief; Jarafi separated us. But I tell you, it was amusing to note that Harold is not the 'tough guy' he has had the entire college believe him to be: The old saying about barking dogs seldom biting couldn't be more true of him!"

"I've never met anyone quite as senseless as that fellow," Sekani said with a shrug of the shoulders after a brief silence.

"Oh, I've met many such people," Andreya said. "In fact, I'm talking to one of them just now."

Shocked that Andreya had spoken in dead earnest, Sekani stopped abruptly. "What can you possibly mean by that?" she asked, knitting her brow uncomprehendingly at Andreya, who was walking straight on as though he hadn't noticed she had stopped. "You've got to explain yourself!" she added, walking towards Andreya, who had now stopped several paces up the gravel road. She could see, however, that her command was unnecessary, for Andreya's demeanor as he stood waiting for her – arms folded over his chest, head tilted purposefully and face stern – plainly indicated that he meant to substantiate his accusation.

"Oh yes, Sekani," he began firmly. "'Senseless' is the only word to describe the way you're behaving with regard to our relationship. You allow yourself to be so attached to me that the whole college thinks we're lovers – as witness Harold's blunder. Yet up to now I've no idea what you really feel about me, since you've stubbornly refused to verbally let me know your feelings."

"But that's not exactly true, Andreya," Sekani protested. "I've told you – and repeatedly too – that I don't want to commit myself as more than just a friend." Then she averted her eyes from him and smiled mysteriously.

"And yet what do people see? They see that we're as close as any lovers. Does that make sense? Perhaps I need to say it one more time: I love you, Sekani. Tell me now: Do you love me too?"

"You've said it often enough, Andreya," Sekani said, eyes still averted. "And I've given you the answer just as often. I don't think there's any more to be said on this."

"Oh yes there is!" Andreya retorted. "And it's this: you're not making sense."

"Well, I thought I was," Sekani said, this time looking at Andreya, and smiling the same maddeningly mysterious smile.

"I don't see how you could ever think you're making sense," Andreya murmured. "Anyway, we've walked far enough: let's be getting back."

They turned and began to walk back to college.

CHAPTER EIGHT

Three months later, at the beginning of Andreya and Sekani's last year at Ginezi Teachers College, an incident in a nearby village unexpectedly provided the unraveling of what Andreya had come to call "the Sekani mystery".

Nyemba village lay to the east of Ginezi College, about two kilometres across a stream. It was a sprawl of about a dozen mud-and-grass-thatch houses most of which had small round huts standing beside them which were used as kitchens. It was in one of these kitchen huts that a young mother sat dozing beside her sick toddler son that hot October afternoon.

Now and again, a heavy nod would awaken Nyahara. Then her sleep-laden eyes would glide under heavy eyelids toward the little boy sleeping beside her on a split-reed mat, his tender brow beaded with the sweat of a high fever.

"I hope the hospital medicine will help," Nyahara said, talking to herself. "Do allow me some sleep tonight, Thula."

She reached for a small sauce-like plate that contained a small ball of newspaper wrapping. She took the little ball, unfurled it, and counted the little malaria tablets she had been given when she went with Thula to Ginezi Hospital that morning. Then she carefully re-wrapped the pills and replaced them in the little plate beside her. Returning her hands onto her lap, she yawned as she leaned forward over her out-stretched legs. She was soon nodding again.

Outside, Wotchiwe, Nyahara's four-year-old daughter, was playing in the shade of the kitchen. The village compound was empty except for numerous pigeons ranging around in search of stray grains, or cooing as they mated. The rest of the villagers had left early that morning for a community development fund-raising piece of work in another village several kilometres away.

Inside the kitchen hut Nyahara dozed on. About a metre from her feet, an earthen pot of beans was bubbling away over a flameless log fire. When she was awakened by the next heavy nod, Nyahara noticed a change of tone in the bubbling of the beans she was cooking. Her many years of cooking experience told her right away what was happening: the beans were beginning to burn.

With a little cry of panic, she sprang to her feet, snatched the pot off the fire, and carefully set it down beside the fireplace. Then she stepped over to the section of the kitchen where she kept her pots in a neat row. Grabbing the gourd dipper that was always kept hanging by its long hooked neck from the lip of the water pot, she dipped it into the pot. The dipper went in deeper than she had expected and hit the pot's bottom. Shrinking her dismay, she tipped the water pot and scooped the few drops of water at its bottom. The beans sputtered as she emptied the dipper on them.

Gourd dipper in hand, Nyahara stood in the doorway of the kitchen and called out to her daughter.

"Wotchiwe! Come in here and stay with your little brother. I have to go to the water hole."

"Aaa, not I!" the little girl protested, not even bothering to look at her mother. She didn't want her playing to be interrupted.

"Ugh, come quickly you! Look, there comes your father: He will slap you if you do not come."

"Aaa, let him come and slap me," challenged the little one, paying more attention to her game than to her mother.

Realizing that lying threats were not going to work, Nyahara tried another approach.

"Come along now, my dear daughter," she said pleasantly, half-singing the words. "There she comes, my pretty, pretty little one. I love my Wotchiwe very much. She never disobeys... I've closed my eyes, and I know that when I open them again, my clean and pretty Wotchiwe will be standing before me... My Wotchiwe is pretty as a flower. Her eyes sparkle like a pigeon's. Her waist is as small as a wasp's. Here she comes... Here she comes... Here –"

"I have come, Mother," said the little one, standing before Nyahara. "You will not take long, will you?" she asked endearingly.

"No, my dear one," Nyahara said, entering the kitchen. "I will not be long. You stay in here till I come back, you hear, my child?"

"As if I will go out?" the youngster said, her head hanging on her shoulder as she curled herself on the floor. "I will not go out, Mother, until you come back."

"That is a good girl. If Thula cries you will soothe him, will you not, dear?"

Wotchiwe nodded.

Nyahara dropped the gourd dipper into the empty water pot, hoisted the latter onto her head, and stepped out into the compound. Half-running half-walking, she hurried off to the water hole.

She had hardly reached the water hole when, back in the village, young Wotchiwe spotted the match box which her mother usually took care to hide in the roof of the hut. That morning, however, Nyahara had forgotten to hide the match box. Instead, she had unknowingly left it lying beside one of the pots. Wotchiwe picked it up. Remembering how her mother had once rebuked her when she had caught her playing with matches, she tip-toed to the door and, discreetly hiding the match box behind her, peered out in the direction of the water hole. No sign of her mother yet.

Wotchiwe then stepped out and stood beside the door, leaning against the wall under the drooping eaves of the squat hut. She cast a few more anxious glances towards the path to the water hole. Then she rattled the match box, opened it, took out one stick and struck it. The little roar produced as the match head flared up fascinated her. She held out the flaming stick with her little hand, which was caked with dust and nose-rubbing. Her absorbed watching of the little yellow flame was not even interrupted by her having to sniff in a column of thick greenish mucus that had nosed its way to the edge of her upper lip. She tossed the charred stick away when the flame began to burn her finger tips.

Just then, a huge spider suddenly rustled in the grass thatch above her, giving her a fright. It ran down the thatch until it hang precariously at the tip of one of the overhanging grasses.

"You die today!" said Wotchiwe to the spider, annoyed at the creature for having scared her. Her heart beating fast from the fright, she looked around for a piece of grass. She saw a nice long one just at her feet and, her eyes fixed on the spider, she slowly lowered herself by bending her knees until she picked up the grass. "You think I am one to fool around with, eh?" she asked the spider. "Well, you will see…."

She struck a match and set one end of the grass alight. Holding the grass by the other end, she thrust the flaming end at the spider. The little creature simply let go of its perch, dropped to the ground, and scurried away.

Her eyes following the escaping spider, Wotchiwe was unaware that she was still holding the flaming grass to the roof. Thus it was not until she began to feel the heat that she looked up to see that the edge of the thatch had caught fire.

With a terrified cry, Wotchiwe dropped both the grass and the match box. She ran aside and took a helpless look at the fire, which was spreading/ slowly in the breezeless air. Then she turned and, screaming about the accident, dashed towards the water hole.

As Wotchiwe was screaming her way to the water hole, across at the college Andreya was presiding over a Drama Club committee meeting. At the end of the previous term, he had been elected chairman of the club and Sekani a committee member. That Friday afternoon the committee was meeting to lay down plans for the term.

The meeting had hardly started when Sekani sprang to her feet.

"Look!" she yelled, fear filling her eyes. "There's a fire in Nyemba village. See, that hut is ablaze!"

Andreya and a few other students rushed to where Sekani stood pointing. They looked across to the village. There were the flames, leaping high, licking the air above and then vanishing into a thick cloud of smoke that swirled skyward.

Led by Andreya, the male students were pressing through the door while the girls were still leaning out of windows, uttering sympathetic cries in the direction of the blaze. Then Sekani and one other girl followed hot on the heels of the boys.

The Drama Club members found that they were not the first to have been aware of the incident. Some students who had been reading in the library had also noticed the blaze and were already racing ahead of them down the slope.

Stumbling into the dry sandy bed of the stream, the students came to a halt when a woman's wail suddenly split the afternoon quiet. Then they saw Nyahara emerge from a clump of reeds, a whimpering Wotchiwe at her heels.

"My child is in there!" Nyahara cried out when she saw the students. "Please rescue my Thula, oh people of God!"

"Bring the water with you, *mayi!*" one student shouted over his shoulder as he followed his friends who were racing up the path towards the village.

"Should I?" Nyahara asked, already trotting back to the water hole, where she had left her water pot.

When the first group of students reached the blazing hut, the roof was crackling ominously. Courage failed them; they merely milled around.

On reaching the burning hut, and noticing that the students were taking no action to save her child, Nyahara purposefully set down the water pot. Realizing what she was up to, two students grabbed hold of her.

"Let me save my Thula, if none of you will!" she screamed, thrashing about and trying to break loose.

"*Iyayi, mayi* (No, madam)!" one of the students holding her said, tightening his grip on her arm. "You cannot. It is too dangerous now to try to save your child. Far too late."

"It is not!" Nyahara screamed breathlessly. "I will save my Thula... Let go of me!..."

As the two students tussled with the kicking and clawing and biting young mother, Andreya, Sekani and the rest of the Drama Club group arrived on the scene.

"My child is in there!" Nyahara told the new arrivals. "They don't want to save my Thula. Please save my son, people of God! Oh, my Thula!..."

Andreya looked around the group of students, and then at the crackling roof. He saw the water pot and, taking off his blazer, he strode towards it. Sekani, who had been standing close behind him all along, now wondered what he was up to and followed him. He dipped the blazer into the water and then draped it over his head. Realizing what he was about to do, Sekani took a firm grasp of both his arms from behind and said, "Andreya, don't!" Andreya turned to face her, the dripping garment almost hiding his face. "Don't, Andreya," she pleaded, looking at him imploringly, her eyes wide with anxiety. Then she let go of his arms and broke into sobs: "Oh, please don't go in there, Andreya. It's too late now... Please, Andreya, I can't afford to lose you. I love you, Andreya ... Oh, I love you so much, Andreya... Please, don't go in there..."

Andreya took Sekani's head into his hands. He gently lifted it and looked at her tear-washed face. How he wished Jarafi and Eva were present to witness this! Then suddenly, guilt crossed his face as he remembered that a child's life was at stake. "I'll be all right, Sekani," he said urgently, letting go of her head and turning towards the blinding blaze.

Acting more under the influence of hysteria than anything else, Sekani quickly picked up the water pot brought by Nyahara and hoisted it onto her head.

Andreya did not see Sekani do this; he was busy hunching himself up under the scant protection of the soaked blazer. He drew in a deep breath and, as one student dived in vain to seize him, dashed for the burning hut.

Sekani, the water pot on her head, ran after him to within a metre of the hut. She was about to throw the water on him as he rushed through the door when one of her feet tripped on the other, causing her to fall. Landing about a metre from where she fell, the pot broke at the door of the burning hut. The water ran through the door into the hut.

The blazing roof crackled and sagged. Sekani, who had by now picked herself up, turned away from the terrifying sight and buried her face in her hands. She sobbed a prayer for Andreya's safety. Then, with a horrifying crash that sent a shower of sparks into the air, the roof collapsed.

Clutching under him a whimpering and coughing little bundle, Andreya was crouching through the doorway when the roof caved in. He was almost clear of danger when he slipped in the mud in the doorway and tumbled to his knees. Then, as the wet blazer flew off him at his sudden falling, the smouldering section of roof above the door crumbled onto his back. As gently as he could in the emergency, he sent little Thula rolling away to safety ahead of him. Then he scrambled to his feet and, red-hot coals and ashes pouring down his back, struggled to pull off his burning shirt as he staggered to safety.

The cloud of smoke that had spouted through the door as the roof caved in lifted, enabling the stunned onlookers to see what was going on. As soon as she saw little Thula screaming and kicking about in the dust, Nyahara fell on him with a cry of gratitude. She picked him up and, as if the fire was chasing after her, ran off for about fifty metres before she stopped to examine her child.

Meanwhile, Sekani, followed by two male students, dashed to Andreya and proceeded to tear off his burning shirt. Then the two young men began to slowly walk Andreya to the shade of a nearby house, taking great care as they helped him along not to touch the multiple boils the fire had left all over his back.

Through his reeling mind, Andreya could barely hear Sekani sobbing his name behind him. There were numerous searing pains on his back. Every gasp of breath he took burned like scalding water. Then suddenly, his stomach heaved with nausea. His mind reeled round and round and darkness surged all about him. He passed out before reaching the shade.

CHAPTER NINE

A ndreya pushed back the blue sheets and sat up on the high bed in his Private Ward at Ginezi Hospital. He looked at his watch: It was well after eight a.m.

"My goodness!" he muttered as he climbed out of bed. "Sekani will come any time now." He got dressed and made his bed.

He had been in hospital for three weeks following the Nyemba village blaze. Sekani had looked after him faithfully since the day he entered hospital. Every morning, noon and evening, she walked the half kilometre from the college to bring him breakfast, lunch and supper from the college kitchen. When Andreya's parents came all the way from Mbuyeni in the Northern Province to see him, his mother had come prepared to stay and look after him till he would get well. But Sekani had persuaded them to return home, promising that she would take good care of Andreya. Andreya's parents had been very impressed with Sekani, whom they had met for the first time.

Andreya was preparing to go to the shower room when there was a knock at the door.

"That should be Sekani," he said to himself as he turned the door's knob.

It was her. She was carrying her usual split-bamboo hand basket in which a green doily was draped over Andreya's breakfast of light maize porridge, tea, bread and boiled eggs.

"Hi, Sekani! Step inside." He took the basket and motioned her in.

"And how's the patient?" Sekani inquired with a smile as she sat on the bed.

"Great!" Andreya replied, placing the basket on a small bedside cabinet. "And guess what? ... Andreya enthusiastically clapped his feeble hands once. Then, suddenly deciding he shouldn't tell her just yet, he quietly sat down beside her on the bed.

"What?" Sekani asked.

"It's a bright Saturday morning outside, isn't it? I should have opened both windows..." He rose and stepped over to the farther window, which he had not opened when he got up.

Sekani smiled as she watched him draw back the green curtains and then opened the window. She knew that the weather wasn't really what he had asked her to guess about. She knew he had begun to tell her something, only to change his mind on second thought. Knowing him, she was sure he would come around to telling her whatever it was without her having to coax him. She wondered, though, if it had to do with what Andreya had earlier said he wanted to discuss with her that morning. The previous evening, Andreya had told her that he had an important thing to tell her. Thinking about it now, she wondered whether he had decided to postpone to today whatever he had on his mind because the previous evening she had had to hurry back to college for a debate; Andreya might have thought there wouldn't be enough time for him to tell her what he had to say. It must be an important matter, she thought.

"Well, it's high time I threw some water on this face of mine," said Andreya, returning from the window. He playfully tweaked Sekani's nose and then picked up his shaving bag. "Won't be long," he told her as he turned the knob of the door. "Oh, by the way...." He closed the door again and leaned against it, facing Sekani. "How did the debate go last night? Should the old custom be abolished?"

"No!" said Sekani, a ring of triumph in her voice. "We, the opposing side, won of course! You see, there's nothing wrong with the bride price custom itself. It's a good custom that serves a good purpose. Unfortunately, it has suffered much abuse at the hands of unscrupulous people who greedily look at it as a commercial traffic.

That's the argument we dwelt upon; and it won us the votes – 35 to 20!"

"A comfortable margin," Andreya commented, turning the knob. "Congratulations! That's an interesting topic. I wish I'd attended the debate." He stepped out and closed the door behind him. The clip-clop of his rubber slippers echoed in the long empty corridor as he walked to the shower room.

In Andreya's room Sekani set about laying the top of the bedside cabinet for breakfast. She took the food basket that had been placed on it and put it on the red-waxed floor. Then she lifted the flower bottle off the cabinet and, before placing it on the floor, took a good look at the Flame of the Forest flowers in it. "These are excellent flowers," she said to herself. "They take long to wilt. Since Andreya was admitted three weeks ago I've replaced them only three times." Then she took up the green embroidered cloth that covered the top of the cabinet. After shaking the dust out of it, she held the cloth out before her and looked at it. It was simply embroidered: A lace pattern ran along the four edges. In the centre, a garland of tiny red and white flowers surrounded the words GET WELL SOON. She laughed quietly to herself as she spread the cloth back on the cabinet: She had remembered something humorous about the day she bought the cloth – the day following Andreya's admission to hospital:

"It's a nice cloth," the girl with whom she had gone to the shop to buy the cloth had remarked on their way back to college. "Remember, Sekani: one thing your boyfriend needs at a time like this is reassurance of your love for him. So, whatever you're going to embroider on this cloth, let it be something that will give him that reassurance. I suggest the words 'Our Love Will Not End' in the centre of the cloth." Sekani had simply laughed it off.

When Andreya returned from the shower he found breakfast all set.

"Thank you, dear," he said, sighing feebly as he lowered himself onto the bed, the breakfast cabinet before him. "I have the appetite of a lion this morning...." He was about to uncover the food when he noticed that the doily draped over it was brand new. "So you finished the doily you've been working on lately!" He examined it closely. Baffled, he shook his head and turned to Sekani, who was sitting beside him, going through one of his magazines. "Women must have the brains of weaver birds," he said, as if talking to himself. "It beats me how you can put together such intricate things as doilies. And how effortlessly you seem to do it!"

"Anyone can crochet," Sekani said with a smile as she went on leafing through the magazine. "It only takes learning."

"It would take me centuries to learn the skill – if it's a skill, that is; but I'd rather think it's an inborn instinct you females have...."

Lifting the doily off the food, Andreya nearly jumped when he saw two boiled eggs in a saucer. "Eggs!" he said, patting Sekani on the shoulder. "How wonderful, Sekani! It's months and months since I last tasted an egg. Where did you get them from?"

"Mara's 'child study' gave us some yesterday when we went to see her after class."

"So that's where you and Mara were going when I saw you."

"Where did you see us?" she asked, surprised.

"I was returning from Mussa's shop when I saw the two of you cross the football field and disappear down the slope." He sprinkled a few spoonfuls of sugar on the porridge. "Now, don't ask me what I went to buy at Mussa's!" he said with an enigmatic smile.

"Andreya!" said Sekani in an accusing tone of voice. "I don't care what you went to buy. But I do care about your recovery. It's not wise for a patient to be wandering as far as the Asian shops when he's supposed to be in bed. Shame on you for sneaking out of hospital!"

Andreya laid down his spoon and, placing his hand on Sekani's shoulder, said: "How about this piece of news, darling? Yesterday morning, the doctor told me that I'll be discharged today."

"Really?" Sekani exclaimed, taking both his hands into hers. "Thanks be to God! How wonderful! Did he really tell you that?"

"Yes."

Their smiling eyes danced at each other. Andreya said, "I don't know how to thank you for taking such good care of me these three weeks."

"Oh, don't even mention it," said Sekani, abruptly releasing her clasp on his hands as if annoyed at the very idea of Andreya thanking her for caring for him. "Eat your breakfast, dear." She resumed glancing through the magazine.

"And did the doctor say what time you'll be discharged?" Sekani inquired minutes later as she gathered the dishes into her basket.

"No, but he's seeing me at ten this morning. Meanwhile, I'd like to have a few words with you...." He reached under the bed and pulled out a shoe box. He placed the box on his lap and waited for Sekani to finish putting away the dishes. When she finally sat beside him on the bed, expectant, he slowly and deliberately took the lid off the box and unraveled the white paper wrapping, exposing brand-new black ladies shoes. "This is what I went to buy at Mussa's shop," he disclosed.

Sekani recalled that just before the Nyemba Village fire Andreya had walked her to Mussa's shop, where she wanted to buy some toiletries. That was the day she had seen the shoes. She had tried them on and had liked them so much that she had promised the shop owner she would come back to buy them after getting her college allowance at the end of the month. Mussa had told her he would hold the shoes for her.

Sekani's eyes were fixed on the shiny shoes in the box. They were elegantly styled little shoes made of fine strong leather. The heels were just right for her taste: neither too high nor too low. She recalled that they were expensive shoes, and wondered how much Andreya had finally paid after haggling for them.

Sensing that there was some explanation for the whole thing, Sekani fought back the urge to hug Andreya in gratitude for the shoes. Instead, she slowly raised her face towards his. Their eyes held briefly and Andreya playfully tweaked her nose before she lowered her face again.

"Sekani," Andreya began solemnly, his eyes on the shoes. "Time and circumstances have shown us that we really like and love each other. We've also discovered how similar we are in so many ways. It's therefore very clear that we're meant for each other. Any objections so far?"

A smile twitching the corners of her mouth, Sekani shook her head without looking at Andreya.

"Good. Now, the incident that brought me into this hospital and the three weeks I've spent here have taught us a lot more about each other. My being admitted to hospital has also given my parents the opportunity to know you. I therefore thought that today – this memorable day of my discharge from hospital – would be a most fitting day for me to ask you an important question."

He paused for a few seconds to let what he had said so far sink in. During the pause he thought he could hear Sekani's heart pounding against her ribs.

"Sekani, will you marry me?" he said, turning a solemn face towards her, though her own was still lowered. After a long moment, Sekani lifted her face towards Andreya's. It was as solemn as his. While their eyes held, her hand searched for his. The two hands stayed linked for several seconds. Then Sekani lowered her face again, at the same time letting go of Andreya's hand. She placed her hands on her lap and nodded Yes to his question.

Andreya took the shoes out of the box, re-wrapped them, returned them into the box, and replaced the lid. Then he said, "I now ask you to accept this *chikole* from me, so that we can pave the way for the commencement of marriage negotiations between our two families." He handed her the shoes.

With a broad smile Sekani received the symbol of their intention to marry each other. Then, in an emotion-charged whisper, she said, "A most fitting day for us to do this, Andreya – the day of your return from the very mouth of death...."

She yielded to his drawing her to himself.

CHAPTER TEN

Two years after Andreya and Sekani completed their training at Ginezi Teachers Training College, Andreya found himself part of a huge audience in Bongwe Town Hall one Friday evening. He had arrived in the nation's capital the previous day, after travelling he whole day from Katoto, where he was teaching at the Presbyterian Primary School in that town.

It was warm and stuffy in the packed auditorium that September evening; people kept fanning their faces with the "Miss Dziko 1974" beauty contest programme sheets. From his seat in the centre of the audience, Andreya could see that the auditorium had been gaily decorated for the national beauty pageant. National colours were everywhere, particularly on the raised stage where the competing girls were to parade. Up front, facing the stage at an angle, a dozen solemn-looking men and women sat behind a half-moon formation of colourfully draped tables.

"How many do you recognise on that panel of judges?" Andrea asked George Malisawa, his host in town, who was sitting beside him. The two had been class mates and good friends at Ginezi College. George had decided to teach in his home district and had been posted to St. Joseph Primary School here in Bongwe town.

"Oh, quite a few," George replied. Between the two of them they identified eight national celebrities among the twelve judges.

In one corner of the hall Andreya could see a young man and a young woman, both wearing headphones. Andreya recognized the young man – who was talking away into a microphone – as his favourite announcer on Radio Dziko. The beauty contest was being covered live on the country's only broadcasting system.

Also on hand was the Radio Dziko Band. It was rattling away some light music from its enclosure in one corner of the stage, entertaining the audience as they waited for the beauty parade to begin.

It had all started two months earlier when, just for the fun of it, Sekani and a fellow teacher at Vukula Primary School decided to take part in the "Miss Vukula Urban" beauty competition. The title had gone to Sekani. A few weeks later Sekani had found herself in Katoto Town Hall, competing for the "Miss Northern Province" beauty sash. She had won it. And now she was here in Bongwe Town Hall to contest the "Miss Dziko 1974" beauty crown.

Sekani had arrived in Bongwe two days earlier than Andreya. She and the four Miss Northern Province runners-up drove the 200 kilometres from Vukula in a Ministry of Culture and Social Development van that had been laid on to transport them to the national beauty pageant.

Presently, the beauty parade got under way. The master of ceremonies – a tall, slender young man, neatly clad in a dark suit, white shirt, and black bow tie – began to call the contesting girls to the stage. One by one, the smiling beauties stepped forth from backstage, handbags of various shapes, colours and sizes delicately slung on the crook of their arms. They gracefully picked their way to the centre of the stage, where, curtseying daintily to the audience's uproarious clapping and cheering, they formed a line that radiated glamour. There were fifteen contestants in all – five from each of the country's three provinces.

Sekani's name was twelfth to be called out by the MC. Andreya thought the audience applauded his fiancée's appearance more uproariously than any other contestant's.

"Doesn't she look a winner?" George commented, nudging Andreya.

"Doesn't she?" Andreya agreed, nervously folding and creasing his programme sheet. He thought the floral red-and-white traditional outfit, narrow-bottomed and reaching to her ankles, perfectly suited her earth-brown complexion. He thought her glossy-black hair, innocently short and natural as ever, couldn't have been better groomed. He thought her smile, which lit up her plump face, was genuine and unforced. And he thought the delicate curtsey she dropped as she joined the line was authentic and unaffected.

After the introductory appearance, the competing girls withdrew backstage – one after another. Then the MC began calling them to the stage again, one by one. From now on he was referring to each of them by the number in which she was first presented to the audience.

"Beauty queen number so-and-so!"

The contestant in question would emerge, clad in the same outfit she had introduced herself in. Smiling as if her very life depended upon it, she would walk about on the stage as gracefully as she knew how, taking care to keep her step to the beat of the music being played by Radio Dziko Band. She would then pace towards the panel of judges, curtsey, and stand before them in as winsome a pose as she could muster. Her stomach pulsating from being strenuously held in, she would stand there for a few minutes so as to let the judges appraise her. The solemn panel would study her, taking notes. She dare not stop smiling, as if that was the only consideration by which they were going to judge her beauty. Another curtsey and, as delicately as ever, she would turn around so as to show off her back to her assessors. Then she would take a round stroll on the long, narrow cat-walk that extended from the stage and jutted out deep into the audience. As she would elegantly walk along, beaming her fixed smile, the audience around her would take stock of her looks, shape and proportion. Thereafter, a little more showing off on the stage, and then a curtsey to the audience. And she dare not withdraw backstage without dropping a final curtsey to the venerable judges.

After an interlude of light music by Radio Dziko Band, the beauty contestants were once again on the stage – one at a time – showing off their stuff for the third round. They had changed into different outfits for this round.

Then came the fourth and final round, the last chance for each contestant to try and persuade the judges – and the audience – that she had "what it takes". After a little final showing off, the girls, having been called onto the stage one after another as usual, formed a stiff but colourful and smiling line. Again Andreya thought the audience cheered Sekani's entry more than it did the other girls'.

After the judges had availed themselves of this last opportunity to evaluate the contestants, the girls retired backstage. Then Radio Dziko Band struck up another interlude of easy-listening music.

It was now time for the judges to undertake the task of sifting and sorting the fifteen beauties and to single out the one face and form, the best all-around "looker" of the entire bevy, that deserved the "Miss Dziko 1974" beauty crown. Of course besides looks, shape and poise, the judges were also to consider each contestant's talent. Earlier that afternoon the panel had given each girl an interview aimed at revealing the extent of her talent and intelligence. Now the time had come for the judges to look at their overall evaluation and come up with the girl who possessed that rare combination of looks and talent. She would be declared "Miss Dziko 1974".

Twenty minutes later, the MC stepped onto the stage, in his hand the envelope containing the judges' choice of the five finalists of the contest. As he read out their names, the girls proudly emerged from backstage and lined up on the stage. Three of them were from the Central Province, one from the Southern Province, and one – Sekani – from the Northern Province. Andreya and George were among the many who stood up and applauded when Sekani's name was called out.

After the MC had announced the second and first runners-up (in that order), there was no doubt on the part of the audience as to which one of the remaining three girls had won the "Miss Dziko 1974" title. Certainly Andreya was in no doubt whatsoever, although he refused to accept George's anticipatory congratulations. "You never know," he told his friend as he nervously fingered his programme sheet, waiting for the MC to announce the winner.

"Ladies and gentlemen!" the MC began in a deliberate, intoning voice. " 'Miss Dziko 1974' – is – Miss Sekani Zuza!"

The tumultuous cheering that greeted the announcement was deafening. The entire audience gave a standing ovation as the other four girls on stage took turns to embrace a beaming Sekani. Then, assisted by the two runners-up, a lady official from the Ministry of Culture and Social Development draped a glittering cape around Sekani's shoulders and lowered a rhinestone crown onto her head. The first runner-up then placed the beauty mace in Sekani's hands.

Sekani was then led to a high, throne-like chair that had been placed in the centre of the stage. Seated on the "throne" and flanked by her runners-up, Sekani was not sure whether the tears that filled her eyes were tears of joy or tears caused by the blinding flashes of cameras as an army of photographers battled with one another to take close-up shots of her.

When the photographers' scuffle was finally over, the MC read out Sekani's prizes: a cheque of 400 kwayera*, an air ticket to the country's only national game park, and numerous presents in cash and kind donated by various individuals and commercial companies in Dziko.

---

*The currency unit of the Republic of Dziko.

65

CHAPTER ELEVEN

The following morning, Andreya and his host George Malisawa were awakened by a polite knock on the door of George's bedroom, where the two of them were sleeping.

"Yeees!" George sleepily answered the knock.

"*Alendo akasambe.*" It was Kadzidzi, George's 13-year-old houseboy, informing his master that the guest could go and have his bath, as water had now been boiled for him.

Without waiting for George to relay the message to him, Andreya, who was catching the Vukula bus at seven that morning, pushed back the bed sheets, swung his legs off the bed and sat at the edge of the foam mattress.

George was lying on a palm mat spread on the bare cement floor in the centre of the room, having surrendered his single bed to his guest.

"I don't feel as if I slept at all," said Andreya, yawning and stretching.

"Me either," said George, looking at his watch as he too yawned. It was a quarter past five. "We haven't had much more than an hour's sleep, you know. No worry, though; you can sleep on the bus."

Andreya and George had left the town hall at two o'clock that morning. They had gone to bed immediately they got home; but they didn't sleep right away. They talked about the beauty contest until Andreya realized that George's participation in the conversation had dwindled to drowsy uh-huhs.

"So," George said with a yawn as he unwrapped himself out of the bed sheets and sat up. "What is it like to wake up one morning only to realize that you're the fiancé of 'Miss Dziko'? I'm sure you woke up thinking you had been dreaming."

"Dreaming?" Andreya said with a chuckle, his voice, broken because of insufficient sleep, sounding quite foreign to him. "How could I think it was only a dream when just two hours ago I was talking you to sleep about it? It's an incredibly wonderful feeling, George!"

"She's flying to Nyamnkhowa National Park this morning...," George said wistfully. "What time are they taking off?"

"Ten thirty. And you know what, George? If I had my way, I'd suggest to the organisers of these beauty contests that winners should be allowed to take their boyfriends along on prize trips!"

Staggering with laughter at what Andreya had just said, George went into the sitting-cum-dining room. He turned on his radio, filling the two-room house with music. A rhumba number was playing on a listeners' requests programme coming through from Radio Dziko. The song was "Nakoki" by Franklin Boukaka, a favourite of Andreya's. It jolted him off the bed and set him swaying with abandon to its drummy beat. By the time the song came to an end, he had danced his sleep away. He then went to have his bath.

The bathroom was in a small building behind George's house. It adjourned the kitchen, where George was now chatting with Kadzidzi as the latter bustled about preparing breakfast. Andreya, who could hear them from the bathroom, was very impressed with young Kadzidzi. He considered him an excellent house-boy: polite, respectful, industrious, orderly on the job and neat in his person. He thought of his last houseboy, whom he had fired only the day before coming to Bongwe for the beauty contest... What was the secret of getting a good, reliable houseboy? How could he find one like Kadzidzi?

Andreya had fired two houseboys in the two years he had been teaching. The one he took in first had started off very well. But then he began pilfering. He had to go. That year his half-brother Phyoka was staying with him, attending Standard Eight at Katoto Presbyterian Primary School. Andreya had decided not to look for another house boy; Phyoka would help look after his humble abode. But towards the end of that year Phyoka passed the Primary Leaving Examination and went to secondary school. Andreya had to find a houseboy. He tried a calm youngster in Standard Five. The little one didn't quite satisfy him. Nevertheless, he decided to hold on to him, always hoping for improvement. But if improvement was on its way, it was taking too long. After keeping the boy for only four months, he had to send him back to his parents for gross neglect of duty. How he wished some of the boys in his Standard Three class were a little bigger. He knew dozens of them who he was certain could make marvelous houseboys.

What was the secret of getting a reliable houseboy? How could one get a houseboy with whom one could leave the keys of the house when one went on long trips? On Wednesday, the day before he left Katoto for Bongwe, Andreya had received a letter from his parents. They had written to tell him that they were coming to Katoto the following Sunday evening to sell maize at the produce market there. If he had a trustworthy houseboy, he would have left the house keys with him. Then he would not be rushing home this morning; instead, he and George would have taken a taxi to the airport to wave Sekani off. But, thanks to his bad luck with houseboys, he had to hurry back to Katoto this morning in order to be home when his parents arrive the following evening.

CHAPTER TWELVE

By mid-afternoon the following day, Andreya's parents, who had left their home area of Mbuyeni some five hours earlier, were nearing Majiga bus stop. The day before, Kaneli had hired a friend's ox cart to transport four bags of maize from Mbuyeni to Majiga. If the Vukula-Katoto bus arrived at Majiga in good time, the couple, their eleven-year-old son Lunya, their toddler son Suzgo and their four bags of maize should be in Katoto before sunset.

Kaneli strode along, twirling a bamboo cane that had once been the stick of a large umbrella. A few feet ahead of him in the dusty footpath trotted Nyasato, swinging her arms rhythmically in order to keep a heavy load balanced on her head.

"What's your hurry, Mother-of-Suzgo?" Kaneli asked his wife in his confident baritone. He had noticed that she was walking so briskly that, despite his long strides, he was making an effort to keep up with her.

"Look at the sun," Nyasato said with a pant. "Did you not say the bus passes through Majiga at three *koloko*?"

"That sun is still very high in the sky," Keneli told her reassuringly. "I do not think the time is even two *koloko* yet."

Slowing down somewhat, Nyasato said: "One cannot trust buses: One day they will come early, another day they will keep people waiting and waiting. It is wise to be at a bus stop on time; a bus does not wait for anybody."

Snuggly strapped to Nyasato's back with a length of blue cloth that matched her shin-length dress, little Suzgo snored away as he bobbed to the quick rhythm of his mother's hips. As for Lunya, he did not seem to have enough patience to walk at his parents' pace. He had run ahead to seek shelter from the hot September sun in the shade of a wayside mango tree. There he squatted, careful not to soil his school uniform of khaki shorts and blue shirt, which he had washed with great thoroughness in preparation for the present trip.

They were now descending a slope. Far to the left, about five kilometres across a stark landscape, a range of hills was barely visible in the dense mid-afternoon haze. Through the trees, leafless as if dead in that dry season, they could see the motor road, an obscure brown streak snaking its way from the left shoulder of the distant hill range and disappearing behind smaller foot-hills in the right corner of the range. Nyasato kept glancing at the road, each occasional cloud of traffic dust there causing her heart to leap: for it might be their bus.

"Father," said the energetic Lunya, rising as his parents reached the mango tree. "Who is going to help us put all those bags of maize on the bus?"

"Every bus has a man whose job is to assist passengers with loads like that," Kaneli told him.

"What about in Katoto? Is the place where we are going to get off the bus not far from the school where a-Andreya teaches?"

"Yes, the bus station is quite far from the school where your brother teaches. We will leave the bags at the station. Tomorrow morning Andreya will find some means of getting them to his house. Perhaps he will hire a lorry."

"Katoto! Katoto!" Lunya suddenly began to chant, joyfully kicking his skinny legs backwards, forwards, and sideways. "Here we come, Katoto!... Father, how big is Katoto? How long shall we be there? Please let us stay for two weeks!"

"Two weeks?" said Nyasato with a chuckle. "Children will be children.... What about duties at home? I hope it does not take us that long to sell the maize."

"What duties, Mother?" the little one inquired innocently. "This is not the rainy season, when people work in the fields."

"There will always be duties, rainy season or dry season," Nyasato told him in a what-do-you know? tone.

Humming a local hymn tune as Nyasato and Lunya talked away, Kaneli was looking tenderly at his wife. How like his first wife – the late Nyasato the elder – she looked: small of build, gracefully poised, quite femininely structured.

"Father," said Lunya. "Why did a-Phyoka not come home this holiday? You told me before, but I have forgotten."

Children can have such short memories, Kaneli reflected. Once or twice before, he had told Lunya why Phyoka, Kaneli's first child with his present wife, hadn't come from the Southern Province, where he was attending secondary school. "This is the last time I will tell you," he told the youngster, striking the ground with his cane in emphasis. "Phyoka is spending the holidays at a friend's home there in the South."

Lunya sucked his teeth in self rebuke and said, "Oh yes. I do not know why I forget so easily."

The three travellers were now going up an incline in the path. It was a stiff climb that made their faces stream with sweat in the oppressive afternoon heat. But it was the last climb before the bus stop. At the summit of the hill was the road-side settlement of Majiga. In fact, they were now so near the place that they could hear the rumbling of passing traffic.

"Father," Lunya piped up again. "When is the wedding between a-Andreya and a-Sekani?"

Kaneli smiled at the coincidence. He had just begun to think about that very subject when the youngster spoke up.

"Early next year," he replied.

Andreya and Sekani would have been married earlier that year had it not been for Phyoka's unexpected entry into secondary school the year before. Since he started teaching, Andreya had been building up a savings account for his fiancee's bride price. Sekani's parents had set her bride at 200 kwayera. Andreya had almost reached the figure when the news came of Phyoka being selected for secondary school. Andreya had to dip into the bride price savings in order to send his half-brother to school. The marriage plans had had to be shelved.

Kaneli was pleased that it would not be too long now before Andreya and Sekani would be married. He twirled his cane with satisfaction as he reflected on the part he and Nyasato were playing to lessen Andreya's financial burdens so that he should put more into the bride price savings each month: The four bags of maize they were going to sell at Katoto should provide the money needed for Phyoka's school fees for the coming school year.

CHAPTER THIRTEEN

The Ufulu Transport Company bus was virtually empty when it screeched to a dusty halt at Majiga. Nevertheless, the small group of travellers who had been waiting for it there jostled with one another as they scrambled for the vehicle's door.

"Wait for those getting off," the youthful conductor reproached them in a quiet but stern voice. He was standing guard at the door while those disembarking took their time collecting their belongings or strapping babies onto their backs. "Why so impatient? Can you not see the bus is almost empty? Every one of you will find a seat. Psshaw!" he pouted and sucked his teeth at them as he shook his dust-covered head disapprovingly.

It was not the seats which the travellers were after; they could see quite well that about half of them were empty. Rather, they were intent on *boarding* the bus. That was the last bus going north that day. Who would want it to go without them? Until they were safely inside it, they could not feel assured the bus would not leave them – empty seats or not.

Nyasato and Lunya were among the first to scramble into he bus when the conductor gave the go-ahead. Choosing a seat for three people, they sat down. Nyasato deftly shifted little Suzgo from her back onto her lap. Then she leaned back on the dusty green-upholstered seat and sighed, immensely contented that the danger of the bus going without them was now past.

The energetic Lunya, unable to sit still at length, had barely warmed the seat when he was on his feet again. He went to the front of the bus where his father, with the help of the luggage assistant, was heaving the bags of maize into the bus.

Nyasato was playfully tickling and grinning at a giggling Suzgo when a Teresian nun clad in a grey habit and a matching wimple walked up the bus's aisle and sat on the seat across from her. Nyasato had earlier seen the nun step off the bus and run over to a nearby grocery. Her forehead, Nyasato had observed, showed that she was probably in her late thirties, though her legs and arms were as firmly fleshed as those of a girl in her prime. Her flawlessly feminine figure showed even through the folds of the ample habit.

Nyasato went on tickling Suzgo, unaware that the nun was watching them with some interest.

"There is a happy little man," the nun said, smiling at Nyasato when the latter looked up only to realize that she was being watched.

"Yes," said Nyasato with a somewhat embarrassed giggle.

The nun said, "That is good. It is an indication he has no pain in his body... Not so? Huh? Not so?..." She lisped the words in baby talk as she spoke to the little one, asking the question several times, each time leaning over to Suzgo and clapping her soft hands at him.

The smile that Suzgo had been wearing since he got the last tickle from his mother spread wider and wider as the nun baby-talked to him. It eventually burst out into a prolonged giggle.

Then the nun paused, reached into her handbag and pulled out a packet of big round biscuits. "Here is something to nibble at, jolly young man," she said, leaning over to hand the packet to Suzgo.

"Please lend us the surname, Sister," said Nyasato, her voice touched with gratitude.

"My surname is Bwerani," the nun said, her full, tender lips parting in a sweet smile that revealed teeth as white as pounded maize.

"Thank you, Bwerani," Nyasato said. "Suzgo, thank her for the biscuits," she added jokingly, smiling at her toddler son. "Go on: Say 'Thank you, Bwerani'". But the little one thanked the nun in his own way: a broad smile and twinkly eyes that warmed the nun's heart and made her chuckle with delight.

"My full name is Sister Juliya Bwerani," the nun said. "And you, Mama, what's your surname?"

"I am Nyasato."

Sister Juliya knew better than to say "pleased to meet you" to Nyasato. That 'educated' people's ritual would have no meaning to a village woman.

"You have boarded the bus here?" Sister Juliya asked.

"Yes. My husband and I are travelling to Katoto."

"Oh, are you? Just to pay us a visit in that town of ours?"

"You live in Katoto then, Sister?"

"Yes."

"I see. Well, our son is a teacher at Katoto Presbyterian Primary School."

"Really?". Sister Juliya exclaimed. "Katoto Presbyterian Primary School is not far from St. Mary's Primary School, where I teach.... Now, what produce of the countryside have you carried him? As you know, we town people miss all the good things available in the countryside, particularly wild fruits like *matowo, mundyozi, vifuwu, masuku, mazayi* and *mahuhu*. Whenever my parents come to see me at the convent, I always insist on Mother bringing me whatever wild fruits are in season at the time."

"Andreya likes *masuku* and *vifuwu* very much. But they are not in season yet. So we have only carried a basket of maize flour for him."

"Oh, that is a big help to him, believe me, Mama. Maize flour is vey costly in Katoto these days. There is great demand for it."

"How is the demand for maize at the market? We have brought a few bags for sale."

"Oh, it is even greater than that for flour. You will have no difficulty selling it."

At this point the driver and the conductor emerged from the grocery where they had been having some refreshments. On seeing them, Kaneli, who had been chatting with Magayisa – a friend in whose house Kaneli had kept his bags of maize overnight at Majiga – said good-bye to his friend and, twirling his cane, strode towards the bus, Lunya trotting at his heels.

As soon as Kaneli and Lunya appeared at the door of the bus, Nyasato pointed them out to Sister Juliya.

"There they come, my husband and our son."

"I see," said Sister Juliya. "What's the boy's name?"

"Lunya."

When Kaneli and Lunya reached the seat where Nyasato was sitting, Sister Juliya smiled at Lunya and said, "Come and sit with me, Lunya." She slid along her seat to the farther end, making room for the boy. "Come on!" she insisted in a teasing tone when she noticed that Lunya was hesitating. "You do not want to chat with a girl? Here I am. Come and sit down."

Kaneli, who immediately understood that Nyasato and the nun had made friends, was laughing richly at Sister Juliya's jesting as he eased his tall frame onto the seat beside Nyasato. Grinning mockingly at Lunya, who was still standing in the aisle, bashfully fumbling with a corner of the back of Sister Juliya's seat, he said: "Go on, Soko. What kind of a man are you? Real men are not shy with women."

Kaneli had hardly finished the last sentence when Lunya abruptly dropped onto Sister Juliya's seat, sitting on one buttock right at the end. Humming incoherently as his tongue flicked to and fro over his lower lip, he scratched and rubbed at nothings on the back of the seat in front of him. When the bus suddenly started, lurching into motion, the youngster was thrown off the seat and landed in a heap at his father's feet. Kaneli sternly commanded him to sit down and stop acting foolishly lest he got hurt.

Half an hour later, the steady drone of the bus's engine began to change into a series of sustained whines as Chitsulo, the driver, changed gears in preparation for stopping at Ndudu.

No sooner had the bus pulled up at Ndudu than it was swarmed over by food vendors calling out their various wares below the high windows. There was also the inevitable jostling crowd of people waiting to board the bus. So driver Chistulo took the opportunity to get off the sweltering dust trap and have some fresh air outside.

Little Suzgo was also being bothered by the stuffiness on the bus. He screamed and kicked and scratched, despite Nyasato's gentle and patient soothing and Kaneli's stern commands to quiet down.

"Let me take him out for a while," Sister Juliya offered, rising from her seat. "It's rather uncomfortable in here."

"This is not the first time I have travelled with him by bus in the hot season," Nyasato pointed out as she helped a willing Suzgo into Sister Juliya's outstretched arms. "He has never been as fretful as today."

Cuddling him as she carried him down the aisle, Sister Juliya baby-talked to Suzgo: It is hot in here, is it not? We will go outside and have some fresh air."

Nyasato was peering out the window to make sure that Sister Juliya and Suzgo hadn't gone too far from the bus when she and Kaneli heard the name Sekani Zuza mentioned just behind them. They turned round to see who was talking.

"I think she's the most beautiful 'Miss Dziko' we've had ever since these beauty contests began," a large, well-dressed man was saying, fanning his face with a white handkerchief as he talked. He was speaking to his seat mate, who was also well-dressed and important-looking.

"Excuse me, *mafumu* for interrupting," said Kaneli, politely addressing the two men as 'lords'. "Did I hear you mention the name Sekani Zuza?"

"Yes, you did," the large man replied, a condescending look on his face. "Why? She is not your daughter, is she?"

"Well, one might say she is. She is my son's fiancée."

The large man's air of superiority suddenly gave way to an interested smile. "You are Andreya Soko's father?" he exclaimed, leaning over as he extended his hand to Kaneli.

"Yes, I am," Kaneli said, warmly shaking hands with the man.

"Well, well. I am very pleased to meet you, Mr. Soko. My name is Phiri. Andreya and I teach at neighbouring schools in Mzuzu."

"Really? My wife and I are on our way to see him."

"So this is your wife! How are you, Mama?"

"I am well, Phiri. How are you?"

"'I am tired. Very tired. Last night I travelled all night by bus from Bongwe to Vukula."

Phiri's seat mate said: "He witnessed your daughter-in-law being crowned 'Miss Dziko' for this year. And that means she's the most beautiful girl in the whole of Dziko this year."

"Yes, I went to Bongwe to see the beauty competition," said Phiri.

"What's this you're talking about, *mafumu*?" Kaneli asked in a perplexed yet expectant voice.

"You mean you did not know?" Phiri asked in great wonder.

"You did not know that two days ago... Wait, is it two days ago? What's today?" he asked his seat mate.

"Sunday."

"Yes," Phiri went on. "You mean you did not know, Mr. Soko, that on Friday night Sekani Zuza won this year's 'Miss Dziko' beauty competition held in Bongwe? Surely Andreya told you about it, did he not?"

Kaneli and Nyasato now vaguely recalled that some weeks back Andreya had told them that Sekani was taking part in some kind of competition. They had not taken much interest in the matter. And, although the contest and its results had been big news all weekend, they could not have heard about it, for they did not have a radio – the only way news like this could be communicated in remote Mbuyeni.

After telling them a bit about the contest, Phiri said to Kaneli and Nyasato: "Andreya and Sekani will tell you more about it. Yesterday, Sekani and her runners-up flew to Nyamnkhowa National Park on a sight-seeing trip that is one of their prizes for being successful in the completion. The girls will be in Katoto tomorrow. So Sekani will find you at Andreya's house."

By now the bus was about ready to resume its trip. Sister Juliya returned into the vehicle and tried to hand Suzgo back to Nyasato. But, refusing to part with his newly found friend, Suzgo clung to the nun as if she was his mother and Nyasato an unknown stranger.

"Forget about me, then!" Nyasato jokingly told the little one, who was looking at her with eyes of rejection. "You go with your friend and stay with her at the convent."

Sitting down beside Lunya, Suzgo nestling on her lap, Sister Juliya joked about the two children: "Now I have two strong men! How lucky I am – two strong men to build me a house, grow me food, and clothe me!" The joke made Lunya so bashful that he hid his face in his hands until the driver disengaged the brakes and the bus began to coast down the slope towards Ndudu stream.

Among the people who had boarded the bus at Ndudu was an elderly man wearing a faded bus driver's cap. His name was Magombo. A retired driver, he had several years back been a colleague and close friend of driver Chitsulo's. The two men were about the same age, Magombo being slightly older. Today was the first time they had met since Magombo's retirement. Thus on arrival at Ndudu bus stop, Magombo had hurried straight to where Chitsulo was standing in the shade of a tree. It had been a joyous reunion. Patting each other as they frequently burst into laughter, the two men had chatted away until impatient calls from the passengers made driver Chitsulo realise it was time to go.

As the bus rolled down the steep slope towards Ndudu stream, driver Chitsulo and Magombo continued to chat and laugh heartily. From his seat facing that of the driver, Magombo made expansive gestures as he talked with Chitsulo. The latter would gesture back with his left hand, minding the steering wheel only with his right hand. Now and again driver Chitsulo, much to the dread of the passengers, would take his eyes off the road in order to stress a point to his old friend.

The passengers' worst fears were soon to prove true. Just as the bus's front wheels touched the long, narrow bridge across Ndudu stream, Magombo rose from his seat. He leaned over to driver Chitsulo and, supporting himself by holding on to the back of the driver's seat, began to whisper some confidential gossip into his friend's left ear. Driver Chitsulo, his left hand placed chummily on Magombo's back, was attentively listening to the gossip when there was a loud bang at the left front end of the bus. Almost instinctively, Chitsulo knew that the left front wheel had rolled off the edge of the bridge. He wrestled with the steering wheel. It was too late. In a flash the bus was thrown off the bridge. It turned over twice before crashing on the ravine's rocky bottom twenty metres below.

CHAPTER FOURTEEN

When Andreya opened the door and stepped out onto his veranda, he almost expected to see his parents coming up the steps that led to his house from the road below. He locked the door, rubbed his functioning eye, which was bloodshot with sleep, and blinked at the glare of the setting sun. He stood for a while on the veranda, shading his eye against the sun as he scanned the dusty road below.

Since it was Sunday, the road was almost deserted. There wasn't the usual fleet of bicycles, their bells tinkling at the paper-bag-carrying crowds returning from the market and the shops. But there was no sign of a lady balancing a cloth-wrapped head load and followed by a cane-twirling tall gentleman, an eleven-year-old boy trotting behind them. He looked at his watch and then walked down the path that led to Mwalilino road, which skirted the back line of the teachers' quarters at the Presbyterian Primary School.

Andreya was tired. Since his return to Katoto town that morning from witnessing his fiancée compete in and win the "Miss Dziko 1974" beauty contest in Bongwe Town Hall, he had had but little rest. No sooner had he arrived home than his fellow teachers began to flock to his house to congratulate him on his fiancée's winning the national beauty title. The congratulators had kept him so busy that it hadn't been until two o'clock that afternoon that he had been able to settle down for a nap. He had set his alarm for four o'clock, since he had to meet his parents at the bus station at five. But when the alarm went off, he had reached over, killed it, and had gone back to sleep. It was the hooting of a passing lorry that had awakened him again two hours later.

Walking down the dusty road, Andreya smiled as he thought about what he had dreamed during the siesta: After all marriage arrangements had been completed, a wedding procession consisting of his parents and other well-wishers was escorting *him* to Sekani's village. That was a strange dream, for in Andreya and Sekani's part of the country it was the bride who left her village and went to live with her husband in his village.

"'Mr Dziko 1974'!"

Andreya turned in the direction of the call. It was Ufulu Transport Company bus conductor Chikwama, a close friend of his who also lived in that part of town. Approaching by a bush trail that crossed a running brook just before reaching the road, Chikwama stopped and began to pull up lengths of the crabgrass that grew on the banks of the brook. Wondering what his friend was up to, Andreya stood still, waiting. Then he smiled as he watched the khaki-uniformed young man fashion the crabgrass into a wreath as he walked over to him.

"'Mr Dziko 1974'!" Chikwama said, intoning the words as he stood on tip-toe to place the wreath on the head of his much taller friend. Andreya jokingly stiffened into a regal pose under the 'crown'. Then the two laughed heartily at the dramatization, patting each other and shaking hands repeatedly.

"Congratulations!" Chikwama said.

"Thank you," said Andreya, his long fingers wrapping around Chikwama's extended hand. "You should have been there to see for yourself. It was colourful, to say the least."

"I followed the whole thing on the radio Friday night. You should have seen me jump around for joy when the MC announced that Sekani was the 'queen'!..." He playfully jabbed a fist into Andreya's side. "So, what is it like to be the fiancé of a 'Miss Dziko'?"

"Oh, it's great, Chikwama. I wish I could describe it."

"She and her runners-up are now enjoying themselves at the national park," Chikwama said wistfully, looking up at Andreya's face, which was beaming under the crabgrass 'crown'.

"Yes," Andreya said. "They'll fly into Katoto tomorrow morning. Tuesday morning they leave for Nkhale Beach on the lake. They'll return to Katoto Tuesday afternoon. Sekani will have supper at my house Tuesday evening. And we'll have a great celebration together with my parents that night!"

"Your parents are coming?"

"I'm on my way to meet them at the bus station. Actually, they're supposed to have arrived by the Vukula bus. I was supposed to have gone to the station around four thirty; but I was so tired I just had to take a nap. I'm surprised they aren't here already. But of course your buses aren't always reliable."

"I'm sure the Vukula bus has already arrived; it's very punctual these days. They probably changed their minds about coming."

"We'll find out," said Andreya. They started walking down the dusty road. "I see you're on duty tonight."

"Yes. I'm on the Vukula night service. I'll be back tomorrow afternoon."

"Good. You're invited to the celebration. And don't fail to show up; I want you to come and crown 'Mr. Dziko 1974' with this precious 'crown' in front of everybody." He fingered the crabgrass wreath, which he was now carrying in his hand.

"You can count on me," Chikwama said. "I'll be there."

"Good," said Andreya. Then, stepping aside to the edge of the road, he laid the wreath down in a clump of tall dry grass. "I'll hide it here and pick it up on the way back."

Just then Ufulu Transport Company's station master for Katoto, Henry Sizwe, bathed Andreya and Chikwama in a cloud of swirling dust as he brought his white Peugeot 504 to a squealing halt at their feet. Hastily rolling down the window, he spoke in an agitated voice: "Chikwama, hold the Vukula night bus till I phone from Mwazisi Mission. There's been an accident...."

"Where?" Andreya broke in, holding down the window which Sizwe had begun to roll up again. "Where, Mr. Sizwe? What accident?"

"I'm in a great hurry, Mr. Soko," said Sizwe, shifting the gear lever. "We've just received word that this afternoon's Vukula-Katoto bus missed the bridge at Ndudu stream and plunged into the ravine."

"The Vukula bus!" Chikwama exclaimed, casting a horrified glance towards Andreya.

Almost involuntarily, Andreya slumped limply onto the window of the Peugeot. He felt as if a sharp blow had been dealt him on the kneecaps, paralyzing his legs. Then, slowly straightening up, he stared unseeingly into the gathering dusk.

"Any loss of lives?" Chikwama inquired.

Although the ill-fated bus's conductor – one of the few who had survived the crash – had told him that more than half the passengers had been killed in the tragedy, Sizwe, grasping that the accident somehow affected Andreya, decided not to give them the information. "Conductor Nyirenda didn't give many details when he telephoned," he said untruthfully.

"Mr. Sizwe," Andreya said weakly as he stooped again to talk to the station master. "May I please have a ride? I was expecting my parents to have been on that bus."

Sizwe's feet seemed to melt in his shoes when he heard that. He swallowed and said lamely: "On the Vukula-Katoto bus? Oh, I'm sure they're okay. Climb in, Mr. Soko."

CHAPTER FIFTEEN

Sizwe pulled up the Peugeot beside the signpost at Mwazisi Hospital turn-off.

"I suppose you want to be dropped off here, Mr. Soko?" he said.

"Yes," Andreya said.

Actually, the thought where to be dropped off hadn't occurred to Andreya throughout the twenty-five-kilometre drive from Katoto. He had realized that Sizwe's destination might first be the scene of the accident, another fifteen or so kilometres beyond Mwazisi Mission. But nothing had been said about where he was to be dropped off. Thus he was somewhat alarmed at Sizwe's decision to drop him at the hospital turn-off. He wondered if the station master knew the worst and had all along been hiding it from him. Could it be that Sizwe had been told that there were no survivors in the accident except the conductor who had phoned? Or had he been told that all the passengers were in Mwazisi Hospital, either dead or injured? His fears were heightened by the fact that throughout the trip from Katoto, Sizwe had given vague answers to some of the questions he had asked him about the accident... All the same, he thanked Sizwe and climbed out of the car.

As he walked down the dark road that led to the hospital, he tried hard to alleviate his fears. He told himself that it was possible his parents had for some reason not been able to make the trip. Or, if they had started on the trip, it was possible that they had reached Majiga bus stop after the bus had already passed. Weren't Ufulu buses notorious for their inconsistency in timing?

But despite all efforts to reassure himself, a knot of anxiety was building up in his throat. It grew bigger and bigger as he got nearer the hospital. He was now swallowing hard, occasionally gasping as he breathed with difficulty over the choking lump in his throat.

He was less than a hundred metres from the hospital grounds when the mortuary came into view. In the bright light of a lamp near it he could see a group of people milling around in front of the 'death house'. His heart began to beat violently and his legs felt as if the bones had been pulled out of them.

Entering the hospital grounds, he saw a nurse clad in white uniform hurrying down a well lighted corridor.

"Excuse me, sister!" he called out, running up to her.

"Yes," she said, stopping for him. There was a tone of urgency in her voice.

"About this afternoon's bus accident," he began, striving to sound calm. "Where are the injured? I was expecting my parents to have been on that bus."

"Where are you from?" the nurse asked, looking at Andreya rather strangely.

"Katoto."

"Are you a teacher at the Presbyterian Primary School?"

"Yes, I'm," Andreya spoke slowly and flatly, wondering what made the nurse ask that. And he did not know what to make of the expression on her face when she asked the next question:

"You aren't Mr Soko, are you?" she asked, knitting her brow as though in disbelief.

"Yes, I am." His heart began to race furiously. "Tell me, sister, what –?"

"How come you've arrived so soon, Mr Soko?" the nurse asked, gently interrupting him. "It's not even ten minutes since I called your school."

"You called?" He was plainly agitated. "What was it about, sister?"

"Mr Soko," said the nurse, surprised. "I'm nurse Nkhambule. I phoned the Presbyterian Primary School hardly ten minutes ago. The headmaster took the phone and went to look for you at your house. But you were not home. So I asked him to tell you to come to this hospital as soon as you got home. You mean you didn't get the message?"

"What is it, nurse? Please tell me. Are my parents safe? Where are they? Are they all right, nurse?"

"This way, Mr Soko," said nurse Nkhambule, leading the way up the corridor.

As they passed by the female ward, nurse Nkhambule saw Dr Cowan, the hospital's medical officer, attending to patients inside.

"There he is," said the nurse, speaking to herself. Then she said to Andreya, "Please wait here awhile, Mr Soko. I won't be long."

Dr Cowan was a Scottish missionary. He and Andreya were good friends. They had met several years earlier at a national conference of the Students Christian Organization of Dziko (SCOD). Andreya had known about the doctor long before that meeting, though; for Dr Cowan, who had come to Mwazisi while Andreya was still in primary school, was a reputable physician throughout the Northern Province of Dziko. But it was at the SCOD conference that Andreya and Dr Cowan had really got to know each other. They had since been such good friends that once, on his way from a SCOD annual conference, the doctor had gone to Mbuyeni to see Andreya's family. And Dr Cowan never tired of telling Andreya that any time he came to Mwazisi Mission there would always be a bed for him in the doctor's house.

As he stood waiting outside the female ward, Andreya wondered what it all meant. There was no doubt now that his parents had been on the bus. He wondered why the nurse didn't seem to want to tell him anything, despite the fact that she had tried to get in touch with him by phone. Why had she abruptly left him and gone to talk to the doctor? Could it be his parents had been injured in the accident and the nurse had gone to check with the doctor if it was all right for

Andreya to see them? But he doubted that; for if his parents had only been injured, he didn't see why the nurse shouldn't have told him so.

Suddenly, everything within and around him seemed to be telling him that his worst fears were about to be confirmed. Cold sweat broke up all over his back as a wave of dismay engulfed him. Desperate, he decided to go in and find out about his parents directly from Dr Cowan.

Ignoring the fact that eight p. m. was too late for visitors to enter the ward, Andreya opened the door to the female ward and stepped in. However, he hadn't gone in three steps when he saw Dr Cowan coming up the aisle towards him. The expression on the doctor's face told Andreya everything. Neither of them spoke a word as Andreya let Dr Cowan take his limp hand and lead him to the latter's office.

It was from Sister Juliya that Dr Cowan had learnt that Andreya's parents were among those who had perished in the bus accident. She herself had been critically injured; and Dr Cowan was attending to her when she told him how she and two little boys had narrowly escaped death. She related to the doctor how, when the bus crashed among the jagged rocks at the bottom of the ravine, she and the two boys were miraculously safely walled around by debris from the wrecked vehicle. She told him that like the boys, she too would have escaped with hardly a scratch had it not been for the deep cut in her left thigh which she had received as rescuers were extricating her from under twisted metal.

"Doctor," Sister Juliya had said speaking in great pain as she lay on a bed receiving blood transfusion, "the parents of the two boys have both perished in the accident. But the two orphans have a brother in Katoto. They and their parents were on their way to visit him. He's a teacher at the Presbyterian Primary School. His name is Andreya Soko."

CHAPTER SIXTEEN

L ying on his back in the darkness of his room in Dr Cowan's house, Andreya turned his head to look at the illuminated clock beside his bed. It was ten after midnight. He had been lying there wide-awake for two hours, staring unseeingly toward the ceiling as he turned over in his mind a chain of thoughts.

He was alone in the large multi-roomed house. His little brothers were with Nyamkandawire, the bachelor doctor's cook, in her quarters in the back yard. Andreya hoped the little ones were sound asleep. It had been a rough day for them. He recalled his reunion with them earlier that evening: After Dr. Cowan had broken the sad news to him in the former's office, he had taken him to the children's ward, where Lunya and Suzgo were being kept after receiving treatment for shock. He found Suzgo crying; and, from the swollen eyes and the thin voice, it was clear the little one had been crying for a very long time. The nurse on duty in the ward had told him that twice she had given Suzgo sedatives – to no avail. "He might be able to rest now," the nurse had said as Suzgo, calling for his mother, clung to Andreya like a drowning child. Standing there, surrounded by his orphan little brothers, Andreya had been at a loss what to say to little Suzgo and how to respond to Lunya's bewildered stare.

Feeling thirsty in the warm September night, Andreya got up and went for a drink in the dining room. He poured himself a glass of water from a plastic bottle which Nyamkandawire always kept in the fridge.

As he turned to go back to his room, he saw the huge medical book which Dr Cowan had left lying open on the dining table. The doctor hadn't had a chance to use the book after bringing it to the supper table from his study the previous evening.

Andreya couldn't recall a single occasion when he had had a meal at Dr Cowan's house and the doctor had gone through the meal without bringing a book to the table to look up something. The previous evening had been no exception: Andreya and the doctor had been in the middle of a late nine o'clock supper when the doctor excused himself, went into his study and returned with a heavy volume. Laying it beside his plate, he was leafing through the book when he asked Andreya what were his plans regarding the burial of his parents. The discussion that followed made Dr Cowan forget about what he wanted to look up in the book. They were still talking when Nyamkandawire cleared the table. The doctor still hadn't used the book when later that night he was urgently called to the hospital to attend to Sister Juliya.

Andreya remembered Dr Cowan once telling him that of each important medical book he had, there were two copies: one copy he kept in his office at the hospital, the other in his study at home.

Dr Cowan was in his forties. A head shorter than Andreya, he was an energetic man who always walked briskly, as if he was at war with time. His eyes, deep-set in a weather-beaten face, more often than not wore a sad look, reflecting the human suffering he was in daily contact with. But sometimes they sparkled like a boy's, indicating the man's enthusiasm for life. This was especially the case when he was engaged in his favourite hobby – hiking in the hills around Mwazisi Mission, rucksack on his back. He sent well-written accounts of these adventurous hikes to a youth magazine back in his home country.

About his parents' burial, Andreya had told Dr Cowan that he had decided to ask that they be buried in the mission cemetery. He had told the doctor that it didn't really matter where they were buried: His parents had died with no real home and – apart from himself and his three younger brothers – with no relatives that really cared about them. So it wouldn't make any difference to anybody where they were buried.

Andreya had decided to bury his parents the following day. He had told Dr Cowan that he would spend every penny he owned to give his parents the decent burial they deserved. He had decided that he would have tombstones constructed on the grave of each of them.

"They were wonderful parents," he had told Dr Cowan. "I know it's rather late now to meaningfully reward them for all they've been to me. The least I can do now is seal their resting place with my gratitude to them."

As Andreya had come to Mwazisi unprepared for anything, Dr Cowan had offered to lend him the money for the funeral expenses. The doctor had also assured him that he would take personal charge of all the funeral arrangements. He would get the mission station's carpentry shop to construct the coffins; and he would work with the mission pastor in arranging for a graveside service.

Andreya awoke with a start. He sat up and looked toward the bedside clock. The illuminated hands showed a quarter to one. So it had been little more than a doze. The dream must have began as soon as he had closed his eyes. And how strange that he should dream exactly the same dream he had dreamt during his siesta the previous afternoon back at Katoto: a wedding procession escorting *him* to Sekani's village!

Andreya wasn't a believer in dreams in the sense some of the people he knew were: rushing to a dream book each time they had had a dream to see what it meant. Nevertheless, he did not completely dismiss dreams; for there had been times when he had had experiences which he could clearly remember having dreamt about. For instance, he had on several occasions been to new places which he could almost swear having been to in a dream somewhere in the distant past. What then could this persistent strange dream mean? He thought about his fiancée. Did the dream have anything to do with her, her safety perhaps? He thought of the belief among his people that an accident usually befalls one who has not been informed of the death of a relative or close friend. He hoped Sekani was safe. She was at

Nyamnkhowa National Park that night; and later that morning she and her runners-up in the national beauty contest would be landing at Katoto on their way to the lake shore, the last leg of their prize sightseeing tour.

Andreya was certain Sekani would find out about his parents' death when the girls landed in Katoto the following day. It would be out of character for her to pass through Katoto without at least telephoning him. And since he had phoned his headmaster the previous evening, she would be told the bad news.

Andreya sighed resignedly as he lay down again. He turned over onto his back, gazing toward the ceiling as his thoughts returned to the dream. Whatever its meaning, he thought, it must have something to do with his forthcoming marriage to Sekani....

Forthcoming? The sudden thought made him blink rapidly. He thought of the savings account he had been building up for Sekani's bride price. Despite difficulties and setbacks, and with a lot of help from his late parents, he had managed to save 120 Kwayera. A few weeks ago, seeing he was almost ready to pay the bride price, he had talked with Sekani and they had agreed to get married in March the following year. But now a large part of the bride price savings would be spent on the funeral of his parents. And then there was Phyoka. With his parents gone, Andreya was now without help in the costly responsibility of maintaining his half-brother in secondary school. And then there were Lunya and Suzgo to look after and send to school. He simply couldn't see how he was ever going to pay Sekani's bride price within six months.

But could he afford a second postponement of the marriage? He trusted Sekani. He knew she loved him so much that she would be willing to wait. But she was now a "Miss Dziko"; many young men were likely to approach her with marriage offers now. Postponing the marriage this time would be leading her to very real temptations.

CHAPTER SEVENTEEN

It was four o'clock in the morning by the clock beside his bed when Andreya heard the footsteps of someone passing by outside his room in Dr Cowan's house. He knew it was the doctor returning from night duty.

When the doctor entered the dining room to get himself a drink before going to bed, Andreya climbed out of bed and went to talk to him.

"Is Sister Juliya all right, doctor?"

Dr Cowan, who was still in his white duster, his stethoscope around his neck, shook his head gravely after taking a sip from his glass of water. "She passed away about an hour ago, Andreya," he said with a frown that seemed to make his deep-set eyes – which Andreya could clearly see in the brightly lit room – sink even deeper into his haggard face. "She'd lost far too much blood before reaching the hospital."

Andreya pulled a chair from under the dining table and weakly sank onto it. He placed his elbows on the table and held his head, staring blankly before him. "Poor woman," he said under a sad sigh.

"Go back to bed, Andreya," the doctor said.

"I can't sleep, doctor," Andreya said, still staring vacantly before him. "Except for a brief doze, I haven't as much as closed my eyes since I went to bed last evening. Sleep just won't come."

The doctor said, "I should have given you some sleeping-pills. I'll give you some now. You need your sleep, Andreya." He went to his study.

Andreya wondered if the pills would work. He had never taken sleeping-pills before.

"You can sleep for as long as you want," the doctor told Andreya after the latter had taken the pills. "We'll have lunch at noon."

"I'll set the alarm for eleven. See you later, doctor."

By lunch time that afternoon, Dr Cowan, who despite going to bed after four o'clock the previous night, had started his day at eight that morning, was able to tell Andreya about the progress of the funeral arrangements: The manager of the mission station's carpentry shop had assured the doctor that the coffins would be ready by two that afternoon; and the parish minister had already started contacting his church members, asking them to come to the graveside service. By three o'clock everything should be ready for the burial.

At twelve thirty, the doctor, who liked to listen to the news whenever he could, rose from the lunch table and went to switch on the radio which was sitting in its usual place on top of the sideboard. Radio Dziko was broadcasting the afternoon news bulletin from broadcasting house in Bongwe.

At the end of the fifteen-minute bulletin the newscaster said:

Here is a late item we have just received from Katoto: Miss Sekani Zuza, the young lady who was crowned "Miss Dziko 1974" on Friday, this morning gave up her prize sight-seeing tour in order to attend the funeral of her fiancé's parents. Our man in Katoto reports that the parents of Miss Zuza's finance were killed in yesterday's bus accident at Ndudu in Katoto District, in which thirty people lost their lives.

Miss Zuza found out about the deaths of her would-be parents-in-law when she and her runners-up arrived in Katoto from Nyamnkhowa National Park earlier this morning. Today Miss Zuza was to go with her runners-up to Nkhale Beach in Wenya Bay District, the last leg of their sight-seeing tour which began on Saturday with a flight to the national park.

Our reporter says as soon as Miss Zuza found out about the deaths of her fiancé's parents she asked Ministry of Culture and Social Development officials in Katoto to allow her to discontinue the tour. Then she took a bus to Mwazisi Mission, where the deceased are expected to be buried this afternoon.

Andreya, who had rushed to the radio at the beginning of the report and had kept his ear glued to the set throughout the item, sighed and staggered back to his chair. Then he began to tell Dr Cowan, who confessed that he knew nothing about Sekani being crowned "Miss Dziko 1974", how his fiancé came to be involved in the national beauty competition. They were still talking about the contest when there was a knock at the door. The doctor rose and went to the living room to answer the knock. A moment later he was back in the dining room.

"It's Sekani."

Andreya's heart leapt at the announcement. Surprised that Sekani should arrive within minutes of their hearing the radio report, he was somewhat dazed as he walked into the living room.

At Andreya's appearance in the living room, Sekani rose from the chair in which she was sitting. Andreya felt her warm tears on his shoulder as the two embraced in silent grief.

After expressing her profound sympathy to Andreya, Sekani asked about Lunya and Suzgo.

"I'll go and get them," said Dr Cowan.

There was nothing Sekani could say as she looked at the two boys' bewildered young faces. As for Andreya, he wasn't sure exactly what emotion was responsible for the tears that welled up in his eye as he watched little Suzgo cling to Sekani while Lunya snuggled up to her. The scene made him think of his savings account, which reminded him of the thoughts that had kept him awake the previous night: The very idea of losing Sekani, whom his orphan little brothers had spontaneously taken to as their new mother, seemed utterly unthinkable.

CHAPTER EIGHTEEN

The size of the crowd that came to his parents' funeral stunned Andreya. At first he attributed the huge turn-out entirely to the efforts of Dr Cowan and the parish minister. But it later dawned on him that many of those who came must have heard the radio report and had come to see Sekani. Throughout the funeral he saw people whisper into their friends' ears as they pointed at Sekani, who had little Suzgo strapped onto her back and held one of Lunya's hands while Andreya held the other.

Andreya and Sekani spent that Monday evening at Mwazisi Mission. Andreya, as usual, slept in Dr Cowan's house, while Sekani was put up for the night by one of the doctor's friends, a Miss McQuity, another Scottish missionary who was a nurse at the hospital. But both Sekani and Andreya had their supper in the doctor's house.

Super over, Dr Cowan went to the hospital and Andreya and Sekani sat talking in the doctor's living room.

"Will you leave the children at Mbuyeni?" Sekani asked.

Andreya chuckled mirthlessly at the question. Then he said: "With whom would I leave them there, dear? If there were anybody there who cared for my family, would I have buried my parents here? I know those people will shed crocodile tears when they hear of my parents' death. I've told you that all these years we've lived in that area, my parents were believed to be wizards. Their presence in Mbuyeni was only tolerated; no one really wanted them there. As a matter of fact, I'm going to Mbuyeni tomorrow not because I want to, but only because it's proper to do so. Otherwise it's not even necessary to report my parents' death to those people."

"How long will it be before you return to Katoto?"

"Oh, I don't think I'll be at Mbuyeni for even a week. I predict my parents will be given a child's mourning period by those people – two or three days."

"Andreya!" Sekani exclaimed her shock. "But that's impossible, dear!"

"Darling, I'll not be surprised if that'll be the case. Certainly, no one in that village will be prepared to go through a week's mourning for my parents. Anyway, I should be back at school not later than Sunday."

"I don't have to return to school till next Wednesday. So I'll look in on you next Monday to see how the children are getting along."

"Which bus will you come on?"

"The afternoon one."

Early the next morning Sekani and Andreya and his little brothers were at Mwazisi bus stop. Andreya and the children were waiting for the Katoto-Vukula bus, while Sekani was waiting for the Katoto-Chisika one. Of the two buses, the former was supposed to be the first to arrive; but for some reason, Sekani's bus came first. It wasn't easy to get little Suzgo away from her.

CHAPTER NINETEEN

The old rattle-trap bus pulled up in a cloud of dust at Chakazi bus stop. Sekani collected her suitcase and stepped off. The overhead September sun was pouring down from a cloudless sky: It was going to be a sticky journey to Chitheba Valley.

Gracefully balancing her suitcase on her head, Sekani took the path that led to her home area. Some fifteen kilometres ahead of her she could see the ridge of hills just beyond Chitheba, the long and broad valley that contained Yadi, her village, as well as several other villages. It being the dry season, the hills looked barren, for the trees were leafless and the bush fires had burnt down the undergrowth.

Three hours later, Sekani, dusty and footsore, reached her village. As she entered the compound between the two rows of mud-and-thatch houses, she heard some singing accompanied by the thud-thud of a pestle striking maize in a wooden mortar. This was the only evidence of human presence in the village.

The singing ceased and a young girl emerged from behind a kitchen hut. She looked in the direction of Sekani and stopped.

"That looks like a-Sekani," she said to herself, shading her eyes against the late-afternoon sun. "Yes!..." She broke into a trot down the compound, chanting "*Akuru! Akuru!* (Sister! Sister!)"

Elida, a pleasant 12-year-old with a round face and large, dark dancing eyes, wasn't really Sekani's sister. She was one of three children of Sekani's paternal uncle. Her parents had been divorced in the local court some three years before. The court had ruled in favour of the husband, giving him custody of the children. Elida's father had since gone to seek employment in a neighbouring country. He had left the children in the care of Sekani's parents.

"Where have all the people gone, Elida?" Sekani asked as the girl unrolled a split-reed mat on the veranda of Sekani's parents' house.

"They're making bricks for a new school block," Elida told her, giving more of her attention to smoothing the mat. "Please sit on the mat, *akuru*."

After chatting with Sekani for a few minutes, Elida thought she could hear the chattering of women. She jumped into the compound and looked in the direction of the voices.

"There comes Mother!" she announced to Sekani when she saw three women enter the compound, empty water gourds in their hands, little bundles of faggots balanced on their heads. The little bundles looked funny to Elida, who was accustomed to seeing the village women carrying long, heavy bundles of big firewood that threatened to break their backs. She skipped up the compound to meet them.

"Sister has come," she told Sekani's mother.

"Really?" Nyamoyo exclaimed. Without realizing it, she began to walk faster than the other women.

Nyamoyo was a tall, long-legged woman, very dark in complexion. Middle-aged, she was younger than most women in Yadi village. But her hair was already graying. This embarrassed her, so she had frequent haircuts. And she was an avid snuff consumer. Sekani always wondered whether it wasn't snuff that had given her mother the chronic cough she had had for as long as Sekani could remember. It was a dry, throaty cough that seemed to be a part of her: Everyone in the village could tell Nyamoyo's whereabouts by that cough.

From Nyamoyo, Sekani had inherited her tall, elegant figure. But her brown complexion had come from her father, Pondamare. A stocky man with a broad, clean-shaved face, Pondamare was very light in complexion, a trait his late father had passed on to him. He smoked cigarettes as avidly as his wife took in snuff: Sekani could still recall how during her primary school days she used to hide her exercise books from him to prevent him from tearing papers out of them in which to roll his tobacco.

Nyamoyo was always beside herself with sheer joy each time her only child came home after several months' absence. She had had five offspring; but all of them except Sekani had been 'eaten up by the earth'. And today she had more cause to be excited over Sekani's homecoming. On Saturday morning three days earlier, the headmaster of the nearby Chitheba Primary School, a good friend of Pondamare's, had bicycled the five kilometres to Yadi village to personally bring to Pondamare and Nyamoyo the news that their daughter had won the "Miss Dziko 1974" beauty competition. Nyamoyo could hardly wait to hear it all first-hand, from her daughter's own lips.

The news of the death of Andreya's parents, which Sekani had brought, considerably toned down the Zuza family's celebration over Sekani's winning the national beauty contest. People who came to congratulate Sekani, unaware of what else had happened, ended up offering her and her parents their condolences. In reply to the sympathizers, Sekani invariably bemoaned the fact that the tragedy had struck at a time when Andreya was almost ready to pay her bride price. She explained to the sympathizers that funeral expenses, the cost of single-handedly maintaining Phyoka in secondary school, and looking after Lunya and Suzgo – all these had upset the marriage plans Andreya had made. As a result, she told the sympathizers, she and Andreya had been forced to postpone their marriage indefinitely.

On the hot and drowsy afternoon of the third day after her arrival in the village, Sekani decided to take a nap. She spread a mat in the shade of a tree behind her mother's kitchen hut and stretched herself on it. But before she fell asleep she heard her mother and father return from a neighbouring village, where they had gone to visit a friend that morning. She could hear that they had brought with them Mazgopa Zozi, a man whose village was near the one they had gone to.

Mazgopa was one of Chitheba Valley's wealthy men. His wealth lay in cattle, of which he was known to have more than fifty head. He had accumulated his cattle wealth through the bride prices of his four daughters. He was reputed throughout Chitheba Valley as one who never accepted less than the customary bride price of five head of cattle for his daughters. In fact, for two of his four daughters, he had charged bride prices of six head each, arguing that they ought to be worth more than the average village girl since they had been to secondary school. One of these two girls had been a close friend of Sekani's; and Sekani recalled how she, the girl, had had to break her first engagement because her fiancé couldn't afford the full bride price for her. The other was married to a wealthy shop owner who already had three wives when she had married him. The shop owner had paid the bride price in cash, which Mazgopa immediately converted into six head of cattle.

Pondamare, Sekani's father, highly admired Mazgopa for his success in raising cattle. Three years ago, he, Pondamare, had decided to emulate his hero the only way he could: He had begun to work extra hard in his maize fields, making sure that each year he filled the maize store which he had constructed specially for the purpose of barter. He hadn't had any trouble bartering his first three yields, for those three years had been rather lean years in Chitheba valley. During such years, people with large families exhausted their maize reserves long before the next harvest. It was such people who bartered cattle for badly needed grain. Necessity drove them to offer fine heifers that served their barter partners well. For example, the heifer that Pondamare got for his first maize store had already calved twice, the first time of which it had given him twin calves. The second crop's heifer had calved once and was already heavy with another calf. The heifer from last year's crop was now mating.

Mazgopa and Pondamare sat on the latter's veranda and continued their conversation. Sekani was within earshot of them. She heard the coughing of her mother as she, her mother, entered the kitchen hut, only to come out again.

"I do not know where she has gone," Sekani heard Nyamoyo tell the two men. "I thought perhaps she had gone to the water hole; but the water pot is still in the kitchen. Maybe she has gone to fetch firewood."

Sekani was about to get up when she heard Mazgopa say: "It is all right, Moyo: I will condole with her on my way back. I already saw the pole yesterday, and it should not take me long to cut it. I should be back before sunset."

"Thank you, sir," Sekani whispered to herself. "See you later. Right now I'm very tired."

"She will have returned by then," Sekani heard her mother say. She could tell Nyamoyo had sat down with the men.

"It is a great misfortune, Zuza, Moyo, this tragic death of your daughter's fiancé's parents," Mazgopa was saying. "Such are the wishes of Satan."

"True, Zozi," said Nyamoyo. She grunted gravely and continued: "What has been done, has been done. What else can we say? They were going to get married early next year, our Sekani and her betrothed. But now, they have had to postpone it. You see, Zozi, the young man has no cattle for the bride price. He is going to pay it in the form of money which he has been saving little by little. And what with the low salary of a primary school teacher, –"

"Sometimes, Zozi, I get the feeling our daughter is wasting her time with this young man," Pondamare cut in. Sekani held her breath after hearing these words from her father. "Their marriage has been postponed twice now."

Sekani heard Mazgopa clear his throat and then chuckled. "You do like this young man so much, do you not, Zuza, Moyo?" he said, and Sekani thought she had caught a note of derision in the man's voice. "All this patience!"

"It is her, Zozi; it is her," Nyamoyo said. "It is not that we do not like the young man. But how long is our Sekani going to allow him to keep her waiting?"

"Sometimes I wonder if you and your daughter are not of the same mind on this," Pondamare said.

"What!" Nyamoyo protested sharply.

"Yes!" Pondamare shouted. "Otherwise why do you not speak to her about her foolishness?"

"Please, do not say that, Father-of-Sekani," Nyasato said with cold emphasis. I have spoken to her uncountable times. You know I have!"

"Yes, I know you have," Pondamare said, his voice still high. "And what does she do – she asks you to talk to me about reducing the bride price. Tell me, have you ever heard of an educated girl like her being given away for less than the full bride price of five cattle? Why reduce the bride price, anyway?" His voice was rising to anger pitch. "*Must* she marry *him*? Tell her, will you, that she *does not* have to marry him. She is an educated girl and…" He paused and chuckled grimly. "Ask her this: Now that she has been declared the most beautiful girl in the whole of Dziko, does she realize that she is the most sought-after girl in this whole country? There are many young men of substance who will be glad to marry her now: young men of wealth, who can afford a bride price many, many times higher than what we are asking that young man to pay. Tell her that, and maybe she will come to her senses."

Sekani heard Mazgopa clear his throat again.

"Er, Zuza, Moyo," she heard him say, "I had better continue my journey. The place where the pole is, is rather far: It is there," she imagined him pointing, "right beside that rock you see near the face of Msama hill over there! So I think I had better be going. I might pass through here on my way back to condole with Sekani."

"She'll have returned by then," Nyamoyo said.

Lying there in the shade of the tree, Sekani could easily picture her mother's embarrassment at her father's unrestrained outburst before Mazgopa. If her mother was going to carry out her father's command to speak to her about Andreya, she thought, then she would tell her – without elaborating – that the problem had just been solved. And that would be the truth: The problem *had* been solved. She sighed with relief as she reflected on the decision she had made while listening to her father's explosion.

"And why not?" she whispered to herself.

A few minutes later she was sound asleep.

103

CHAPTER TWENTY

It was Lunya who first spotted Sekani as her bus rolled into Katoto bus station the following Monday afternoon.

"There's sister-in-law!" he announced to Andreya, pointing at one of the windows of the bus.

"Can you see her, brother? There, through that window."

"Where's Suzgo?" Sekani asked Andreya as soon as she stepped down from the bus.

"Suzgo's sick," Lunya answered the question as he took hold of Sekani's hand. "He's sleeping at the house."

"Nothing serious, dear," Andreya reassured Sekani. "He got up with a mild fever this morning."

"Poor boy," Sekani said. "So you managed to find a houseboy already?"

"No, I don't have a boy yet."

Sekani's eyes shot up at Andreya's face accusingly. "Then why didn't Lunya stay home with Suzgo, dear?" she demanded.

"He'll be okay; he's not that bad. And he's a good sleeper."

"A patient should never be left untendered. You did take him to hospital, I hope?"

"Yes, of course."

Andreya climbed the bus's ladder and brought down Sekani's suitcase from the luggage rack. He hoisted it onto his shoulder and led the way out of the not-so-crowded bus station.

Suzgo was still sound asleep when the three reached Andreya's house. After Andreya and Sekani had had half an hour's chat, during

104

which they shared their experiences over the past week, Sekani went into the kitchen and set about preparing supper, while Andreya and Lunya walked over to the nearby township market to pick up some onions and tomatoes.

As she pottered about with the kitchen tasks, Sekani turned over in her mind thought after thought. She hadn't told Andreya what she had heard her parents say that afternoon the other day. There was no reason to tell him such things, especially since everything had gone fine after that outburst from her father: Following Mazgopa's departure, Nyamoyo had picked up her water pot and had gone to the water hole. Pondamare had slung his axe on his shoulder and had left for the bush to cut some poles with which to repair a breach in the cattle stockade. Neither of them had seen her sleeping in the shade of the tree behind the kitchen hut. Nor had Mazgopa returned to the village.

Nyamoyo, of course, had not spoken to Sekani as her husband had urged her to. Sekani had known from the start that her mother wouldn't say to her the sort of things Pondamare had suggested that afternoon. True, Nyamoyo shared Pondamare's anxiety concerning the future of her relationship with Andreya. But that was all. As for her father, it was clear to Sekani that his attitude towards her relationship with Andreya was influenced by greed. Plainly, her father's desire to accumulate cattle wealth had blinded him to reason and understanding. That thought brought back to Sekani's mind the greed she had seen in her father's eyes when he had suggested to her that the best way to invest the money she had acquired through winning the beauty competition was to buy cattle....

Suzgo's coughing from Andreya's bedroom interrupted her train of thought. She dried her hands and went to check on the little one.

Suzgo was already awake when Sekani entered the room. As soon as he saw her, he sat up and smiled at her.

"Hallow, a-Soko!" Sekani said, lifting him off the bed. "Are you feeling better? Huh, a-Soko?" She touched the tender brow. Suzgo smiled and clung to her. "Yes, you are feeling better. Good. Do not be sick, now; we do not want you to be sick. You hear that, a-Soko? Do not be sick."

During supper, Sekani said to Andreya : "I'd love to take Suzgo with me to Vukula tomorrow if you'd let me."

"I'd be glad to let you, Sekani dear," Andreya said. "But Phyoka will be coming any day this week. I think Suzgo should be here when he comes."

"He most certainly should," Sekani agreed. "I should have thought of that... I wish I could stay longer and help with the children. But I really have to go back to school. I hope you find a houseboy soon, dear."

"Finding a boy is no problem in this place. The problem is finding a good one."

Later than evening, after Lunya and Suzgo had been put to bed, Andreya and Sekani sat talking at the dining table. At one point during their conversation Sekani reached for her handbag and took out a sealed envelope. She handed it to Andreya.

"That's your share of the beauty contest 'manna-from-heaven'," she told him with a smile. "Sorry I couldn't give you more than that. The old man lectured me on what a good investment cattle are; so I promised to send him a few kwayeras for three or four beasts. He –"

"Stop it, Sekani!" Andreya interrupted her with a laugh. "You don't have to render account of how you're going to spend the money. It's your money...."

He slit the envelope open. Inside were a note card and a cheque. He read the note before looking at the cheque: *To you, darling. With love. Sekani*. Then he pulled out the National Bank cheque. He took one look at the amount on it and then, quietly and deliberately, put it back into the envelope. He placed the envelope on the table and looked at it for a long moment. Then he looked at Sekani's beaming face.

He did not smile back at her. Sekani's face suddenly froze. She wondered what was wrong. Her smile returned when he reached out his hand across the table towards her. But her face became a blank again when she noticed that he still didn't return her smile. Solemn-faced, Andreya clasped both her hands into his and said:

"I don't know how to thank you for this gift, darling. All I can say is, it's an answer to prayer. God knows how much I dreaded the very thought of postponing our marriage again. If I needed you in my life, Sekani, now I also need you – badly need you – *in my home*...."

That's what the gift is intended for, Sekani thought as she looked at Andreya's face which was now creasing into a broad smile.

Andreya rose and went to Sekani's side of the table. He took her by the hands and swept her off the chair on which she was sitting. They hugged.

CHAPTER TWENTY-ONE

Yadi village's water hole was in a clump of evergreen katope bushes above which the branches of a giant mukuyu tree spread like a huge umbrella. Although it belonged to Yadi village, the water hole was shared by several villages in the neighbourhood, some of which were as far as five kilometres from it: Water was a big problem in Chitheba valley during the dry season.

Nyamoyo was used to walking down the path to the water hole in the heat of an October mid-afternoon like this one. As she padded along in the sun-baked dust, her toughened bare feet didn't seem to mind the heat. Even the cicadas in the trees overhead, with their shrill rasping shrieks that seem to mock one as one travels unsheltered from the blazing sun, did not seem to bother her. Her empty water pot precariously balanced on her head, she trotted along, preoccupied with thoughts of how best to tackle the hundred-and-one household tasks that were yet to be attended to that day.

As Nyamoyo hurried along, down at the water hole two Yadi women who had preceded her gossiped:

"Have you heard, Mother-of-Baryenge?" said one of the women, shouting from the bottom of the deep water hole to her friend, who sat a few metres from the rim of the hole, awaiting her turn to draw water.

"Eh?" said mother-of-Baryenge. "What is it, Mother-of Nengezi?"

"Aaaah, you will not believe this. The way children behave these days makes one's head spin. I do not know what the world is coming to...."

The woman outside the water hole waited. But for the next several seconds all she heard from within the water hole were the regular gurgling sounds as her friend poured into her water pot dipperful after dipperful of water scooped from the scanty pool at the bottom of the well.

"Speak then, Mother-of-Nengezi," said Mother-of-Baryenge, shouting to the woman in the well. "What is it?"

"It is a veritable *munthondwe*, Mother-of-Baryenge. That is what it is: a portent."

"Tell me about it then, Mother-of-Nengezi," urged the woman outside the water hole.

"Well, when was it? Two weeks ago, was it not?"

"When what?"

"When the go-between in Sekani's marriage brought the bride price."

"Yes, it was two weeks ago."

"Well, you remember how everybody doubted that there was ever going to be a marriage between Sekani and her betrothed at Mbuyeni?"

"Yes. The Sokos were failing to bring the bride price."

"Well, you remember that the young man's parents died recently?"

"Yes. In a bus accident."

"Well, you remember that recently Sekani won some competition and received a lot of money in prizes?"

"Yes."

"And you remember that last week the go-between on the Sokos' side brought Sekani's bride price?"

"Yes. It was money, not cattle."

"Well, that money was from none other than Sekani. Sekani herself gave the money to her betrothed. Then the young man had it brought to a-Pondamare as Sekani's bride price." For good measure, Mother-of-Nengezi spoke these words in a sing-song voice.

"What are you telling me, Mother-of-Nengezi?" Mother-of-Baryenge shouted incredulously. "Are you saying that the money the go-between brought was given by Sekani *herself* to her betrothed: and then the money was treated as bride price *for her*?..."

Just as Mother-of-Baryenge began to exclaim her incredulity to her friend in the well, Nyamoyo reached the edge of the water hole thicket. On hearing her daughter's name, Nyamoyo stood still and listened attentively, hidden from the other two women by the dense foliage of the evergreen bushes.

"So they say, Mother-of-Baryenge," sang Mother-of-Nengezi. She was now climbing out of the water hole by the wooden ladder that had been placed against its wall. Her friend had now stood up, unable to sit still after having heard such exciting news.

After she had emerged from the water hole, Mother-of-Nengezi went on: "Am I one who believes in hiding things? No, I am not. Therefore I will tell you from whom I heard this: I heard it from a-Nyasiliva of Kayaya village. Mother-of-Bezulu and I found her drawing water here this morning. She told us that she had heard about it from a-Nungu, the bamboo-basket hawker from Katazuka village in the hills. A-Nyasiliva said a-Nungu had told her that the news had come to Katazuka village from Kamembe village, where the go-between *himself* is said to have confided to friends about it."

"Mm!" grunted Mother-of-Baryenge, clapping her hands once with a muffled thud – an indication of utter bewilderment. "It means Sekani has paid her own bride price, that is what it means. A girl furnishing her own bride price! An unheard-of thing! Truly, this is a *munthondwe.*"

"Truly, Mother-of-Baryenge, it's a *munthondwe.*"

After Mother-of-Nengezi and Mother-of-Baryenge had exhausted the gossip, Nyamoyo stepped out into the open. A tense atmosphere surrounded the water hole as soon as Nyamoyo joined the two women. It was as if the other two women knew that Nyamoyo had been listening to their gossip. The tenseness lingered among the three women, affecting their conversation till one by one they returned to the village.

CHAPTER TWENTY-TWO

"Nyamoyo!" Pondamare called her just as she was setting down the water pot in its usual place in the neat row of pots in her kitchen hut.

"Baba!" Nyamoyo answered the call and went to the veranda of the main house, where her husband was lounging on a folding chair. She curled herself on the floor before him.

"We have received another letter from Sekani," Pondamare told her.

Nyamoyo noticed a faint smile on her husband's lips.

"Aa?" she said. "It is the wedding notice this time, is it not? The letter we got from her last week said we should be receiving the wedding notice this week."

"Yes, it is the wedding notice. They will be married on 24 October. That is – let me see… That is in three weeks' time. They will be married in the Presbyterian Church there in Katoto, and the celebrations will take place at son-in-law's school. She says she has already posted the money for our transport to the wedding…" Then he laughed – a brief, self-conscious laugh.

"What is it?" Nyamoyo inquired about her husband's laughter.

"You heard what Mother-of-Nengezi and Mother-of-Baryenge said at the water hole.

It was Nyamoyo's turn to laugh – the same brief, self-conscious laugh.

"You also heard them, then?" she asked.

"I heard everything. I was returning from cutting some poles for the cattle stockade. Through the woods I could see you listening to them too."

There was a brief awkward silence. Nyamoyo broke it:

"Yes, I heard what they said," she said quietly.

"What do you say about it?"

Nyamoyo was surprised at her husband's composure.

"Well," she said. "They will gossip, and they will laugh. But everything is settled now, Father-of-Sekani. Things cannot be reversed now."

"Who said things should be reversed?" said Pondamare in a voice much calmer than Nyamoyo had expected. He was gazing past her at the distant hills while his right hand fumbled for tobacco in one of the pockets of his heavily patched khaki trousers.

A cow mooed in the distance. In the dry season, cattle in Chitheba were left to roam untended, as there were no crops in the fields.

"These cattle have wandered too far today, Pondamare said. "The sun has almost set, yet none of them is home. I suppose I had better go and fetch them."

"Father-of-Sekani," Nyamoyo began. Her eyes were downcast, but she spoke with quiet courage: "I know people will laugh. But I hardly blame Sekani for what she has done..." She paused, waiting for an outburst from her husband. It did not come. She went on: "If I had to blame anybody for this, I would blame us – you and me. I have always felt that affection between a boy and a girl is a very important factor in these matters. It ought to be taken into consideration. If we had realized this from the start, we should not have insisted on the full bride price, despite the fact that we knew the hardships our son-in-law was facing."

Throughout Nyamoyo's little speech, Pondamare's eyes were fixed on the tobacco he was rolling in a piece of paper. Then, gazing into the distance while he licked the edge of the piece of paper so that he could seal the cigarette, he spoke over his tongue, saying: "I suppose you're right.... Go and get fire for my cigarette...."

Nyamoyo rose and walked over to the kitchen hut. She walked lightly, as if a heavy load had just been lifted off her head.

Printed in the United States
By Bookmasters